Evernight Publishing

www.evernightpublishing.com

Copyright© 2015

Allyson Young

Editor: Jessica Ruth

Cover Artist: Jay Aheer

ISBN: 978-1-77233-487-6

VANQUISHED

Allyson Young

Copyright © 2015

Chapter One

The shudder of the big ship threw her from her bunk, and Neira Grekov rolled across the narrow floor space before coming up short against the stack of cabinets holding her meager belongings. She sucked in a draught of air against the bruising pain in her shoulder and hoped the drawers wouldn't open and tumble their contents on top of her when the ship actually yawed this time. Vessels this size shouldn't *flinch*.

A reaction of this nature could only mean an attack, and her body reacted both atavistically and in the manner it had been trained—not such a dichotomy as one might expect. She curled in on herself, drawing up her legs and folding over her arms to protect her vulnerable organs and head even as her mind searched for a more aggressive manner to react, then accepted her current defensive position was the best she could assume at the moment.

"Lights." Forcing her voice to sound crisp and collected, the word passed dry lips, her mouth sour with adrenaline.

The room lit in blind obedience, both the overhead lights and lamp by the bed turning on before they flickered into emergency mode. But it was enough to see, and Neira braced against the cabinet, tugging open the drawer to her left, managing to secure a pair of leggings and her loose black tunic.

As the ship shuddered to a dead halt, evidenced by the shifting in the gravitational integrity, she held herself hard with the expectation of being set adrift, but the field held. Wasting no time attempting to analyze a situation she was hardly experienced in as a passenger, Neira yanked her nightwear off over her head and struggled into the clothing she'd procured. She blessed the fact she'd worn briefs to bed, and if her breasts were unbound beneath the shift, at least the material was opaque. A bound chest was better for combat but perhaps this precipitous event wasn't going to involve any form of fighting. With a grimace, she shoved that hope down— her luck didn't run that way.

Crawling toward the door, she searched for the small satchel holding the weapons of her previous trade, and the relief upon finding the bag offset the impetus of the adrenaline, making her momentarily weak. She felt carefully into the wide mouth and extricated a sheath containing her favorite dagger, then found her *palka*. The short, heavy piece of hardwood, long since extinct on the Home World, fit into her hand in a manner akin to a lover's cock. Irreplaceable, it had been passed down through the generations in her family, and she'd be the last Grekov to honor it. She had little enough to take with her to her destination but couldn't leave her weapons behind, not when they'd been thoughtfully retrieved by the team that had found her and Petrov.

A memory flickered and she easily suppressed it, focusing on touch, scenting the stale recycled air of the vessel and waiting for the next unexpected event. The ship groaned like a live thing as it recovered its equilibrium. Neira allowed herself a moment's hope. Perhaps it had been a collision with a rogue asteroid or an accident with the new star engines, rather than an attack. Well, there was no point in hiding in her quarters like a cornered rat in the more likely event that her optimism was futile. She stood, grateful for the correction of her inner ear perception, and hit the control that opened the door to her quarters, taking care to stand well to one side.

Instead of sliding open with its usual alacrity and accompanying hiss, the heavy panel inched aside with a grating sound, the tiny increments of corridor it revealed making Neira's pulse spike. Drawing on her past training, she calmed herself. She ensured her dagger was secured at her hip and hidden by her tunic, then hefted the *palka*. She nearly laughed with the release of tension when the door opened fully and there was nothing but the dimly lit hallway to be seen.

Stepping out, she looked first right, then left. The biggest threat, if there was one, would come from the right where the lift was located. Nothing. She ran lightly in her bare feet along the heavily gripped floor. The material sprayed there and halfway up the walls was an excellent deterrent to slipping and falling, but it was a horrible surface to pull or push luggage along. Wheels and fabric alike tended to catch on the material and bring the owner up short. Boots, anything with gripped soles, almost guaranteed a twisted ankle, hence her bare feet. But then, the *Astris* had been first and foremost a troop ship, hauling those men and women bearing duffel bags to offload them in far off places, the better to protect the Home World's interests in this part of the galaxy. The politicians now appeared to believe previous possession meant nine-tenths of the law and set up settlements on those interests even after learning the hard way that archaic rule didn't necessarily apply any longer.

In any event, the *Astris* had been transformed into a passenger liner, carrying workers to planets still held by the Home World. Mechanics to manipulate and maintain the machinery that mined some of those planets. Workers to replace and support those who toiled on the farms. This wasn't a luxury transport, but the people it carried didn't possess the packs and weaponry of the former passengers, and Neira thought the owners might have spent a few more notes on basic comforts.

Her brain allowed the vagrant thoughts as she neared the lift, mentally discarding the usual noises of the *Astris* learned over all these weeks on board, now homing in on the others—assessing foreign sounds. Thumps, a faint ring of steel against steel, the distinct hollow *crump* of a phase weapon—*inside* a fucking space ship! Fear cramped her belly and she picked up the pace. Someone was either really stupid or desperate. Neither assessment boded well.

Other panels along the corridor opened. She could hear them behind her, and two ahead, starboard, hitched wide. A woman's head poked out of the first, a man's from the second and Neira halted, her feet squeaking audibly against the floor's surface.

"Do you have weapons? Training?" She snapped out the questions, and the wild-eyed regard of both of her fellow passengers became focused.

"No. I'm a farmer," the man said. She'd seen him around, in passing. Yuri somebody.

"Same," answered the woman. She was a young, pretty blonde, and fear twisted her features. Victoria, or Vicky. Neira liked her from what she had gleaned during their brief conversations at meals. Not impressed with herself, despite her beauty and attractive figure, and ambivalent about her destination. Most everyone on the ship appeared to be, but there was little enough to keep them on the Home World.

"Then stay inside and lock up. We've either been boarded, or someone's lost their fucking mind. I heard a phase weapon."

Blinking, Yuri nodded and withdrew. Vicky followed suit but far more slowly. Civilians. Neira wondered if she should stay on this deck and guard them until the ship's escort noticed they had lost their plump sheep and flew to the rescue. If her instincts were correct, the *Astris* was under attack, and probably from pirates. The only thing those cursed beings were interested in was booty.

They'd take the shipments intended for the colonies. The healthiest and strongest of the men would be sold as work slaves. If they were lucky they'd be sold to the Shadalla, although with the treaty that alien race could now offer gainful employment, so perhaps there were other buyers that didn't immediately come to mind. The rest of the men might be murdered or left on a crippled ship to fend for themselves. The women... Neira had heard tales about the pirates, and after discarding the usual seventy-five percent of embellishment, she was still appalled by what she recalled. The abuse and torture... Another memory flickered and this time surged to the surface. She battled it back, swallowing against the bile. Her face twisted in response. She thought she'd become adept at repressing.

Thinking again about the female passengers, Neira recalled the briefings by her commanders. There was evidence the Shadalla also bought and kidnapped women in the past and were said to crave Home World females. None had ever returned, despite the treaty. Neira didn't know if that was because they chose not to, or weren't able. She'd be inclined to believe the latter. Her past experiences had polished her natural cynicism into a sharp, ever-present reminder.

Turning back to survey the other people cautiously peering from their quarters, she asked the same questions of them—could they arm themselves and fight with her? Negative headshakes answered her and she told them to take cover and lock down. Primarily women, all but one followed orders. The slight form pattered toward her, unfettered breasts bouncing beneath the loose fabric of night apparel, and with a broken off lamp base clutched tightly in one hand.

"What's going on?" It was Toya, introduced as a master mechanic and destined for the far planet of Bloor where the environmental machinery was giving them fits. Neira had heard Toya's musings and plans for repair often enough, having also met her during meals or the long walks around the decks most took to stave off excruciating boredom. Neira walked to keep fit when she wasn't exercising in the privacy of her quarters, not for socialization, but she was forced to mingle sometimes. Toya seemed to want to interact with her more than the others.

Surveying the improvised weapon, the connective wires removed and the heft already making the smaller woman's arm droop despite the wiry muscles developed by her profession, Neira couldn't help but experience a glimmer of humor. It was tempered by admiration that Toya didn't plan to go down without a fight. In truth, she hadn't found much to like or admire about the master mechanic, who was far too nosy and intrusive for her taste.

"I think we've been boarded. Attacked, certainly." She referred again to the phase weapon.

"On board?" Toya's voice was incredulous and

her green eyes grew enormous. "Are they fucking nuts?" Perhaps Neira wasn't the only one who'd spent time among the rough and ready.

"I'm gonna stand watch at the lift until I can raise somebody in charge." *If there is anyone in the ship's roster left,* Neira thought grimly. Apparently Toya had the same thought.

"If it's pirates, they'll be routing the bridge, taking control. We should make our way to the pods, get off while we can." Toya shifted her weapon to the other hand as she scrutinized the *palka* intently.

"They'll pick us off."

"Not all of us. You should come and we'll ask some others to take pods too. It'll make killing all of us more difficult." The redhead bounced on her toes.

So Toya wasn't a hero. Smart girl. And Neira wasn't either, not anymore. But the idea of running didn't appeal. She knew whoever was ballsy enough to attack a Home World vessel wouldn't scruple at destroying or disabling all the pods to keep anyone from escaping and telling the authorities the fate of the *Astris*. She'd rather go down fighting than imploding in space or suffocating from lack of oxygen. Toya obviously had something to live for, and Neira winced at the bite of envy. Maybe one pod wouldn't be noticeable.

"Suit yourself. I'll take my chances here." She gestured Toya away.

Visibly hesitating, the little redhead changed her grip on the lamp base. For an incredulous moment, Neira thought Toya meant to *strike* her. She shifted automatically into defense mode. Then the other woman relaxed. "Okay. I'm going. I'm not attached to any of my possessions. I'll make do with what's in the pods."

Neira watched as Toya ran awkwardly in the opposite direction, overbalanced by the makeshift weapon, to where a few of the emergency transits were fitted into the bulkheads. She struck each door of the cabins with the heel of her hand as she passed, and several edged open, the occupants' heads poking out of the openings at various heights.

"I'm taking a pod," she called out as she ran.

Almost as one, the heads turned to look at Neira, who stood without giving them anything. They should make their own choices. She didn't command any longer, having lost that privilege in the most vile manner possible. Some with a shake, others without any noticeable response, they all withdrew in jerky increments. Toya gave Neira a look over her shoulder that she couldn't interpret. She wished the other woman luck with a stare of her own.

Turning her attention back to the lift doors, she then longed for cover, feeling as exposed as a *ryba* out of water. Though that probably wasn't an accurate analogy. *Rybas* tended to adapt quickly, their multichambered lungs capable of breathing both air and fluid. Neira thought she might be drowning.

Anxiety mounting, she peered forward and believed she heard the faint whine of the turbos that dropped the lifts between decks. There had been no announcements. No reassurance from the captain. It was too much to believe there had been such widespread malfunctions that all the communication options were neutralized. So it had to be pirates. Fuck. Maybe she'd given the wrong impression by remaining neutral. Maybe she should have told everyone to head for the pods. Her faith in her ability to command and make good decisions had been so shaken by past events. Unbidden thoughts threatened to flood her brain and immobilize her, and Neira automatically practiced the techniques the therapist had taught her. *Concentrate on your feet, remain grounded, feel your surroundings, know you aren't back in that place. Breathe.*

Slowly the sensation of breathing underwater eased as the tested approach kept her in the present as usual, and while the hair at her temples grew damp and her chest ached, it was enough to push past the trauma and gain control of her body. Neira reapplied her focus to the situation. All she had left was to try to make this a choke point, give any other survivors a chance to fend off those attempting to gain access to their cabins. Maybe buy some time for the Outriders—those smaller but well-armed and nimble craft—to return and engage the pirates and drive them off. Hope was all she had.

The policy of sending those escort ships racing ahead to clear space, instead of tending the slower vessels like *Astris*, was another foolish choice in Neira's opinion. She might not understand astrophysics or gravity infusers, but she did grasp the art of war and the techniques contained within that art. And her opinion had just been supported. The passenger ship was indeed like a fat ewe for the plucking, no matter they weren't supposed to be at war with anyone any longer. A few Outriders should have been left behind. *Der'mo*. Not that cursing in her native language was going to change anything, except everything did appear to be going to shit.

A panel worked open behind her and she whirled, weapon at the ready, too wired to mute her trained response. Yuri emerged, a closet support rod in his hand and a determined look on his Slavic features. Neira wondered if he saw a similarity in her own facial structure as his gaze met hers. They had never exchanged last names—people on vessels like these rarely connected for more than polite social necessities, loners almost always without exception, although she suspected Toya had had an affair with one of the crew.

13

"It is pirates," Yuri announced, clearly having thought things through. When she didn't attempt to dissuade him, he asked, "What's your plan?"

"Hold them at the lift, block the doors, anything to give our escorts time to figure it out and get back to save the day."

Yuri arched a brow at the bitterness in her tone but didn't respond to it. He nodded, then looked at the doors and back at her. "How?"

"If they use a phase weapon we're fucked. But I can't think they'd be so stupid. It was probably one of the crew who objected to being cut down, slaughtered."

"You think the crew…" Yuri's face paled even more and his Adam's apple bobbed as he swallowed hard.

"I don't think anything, really. I don't *know* anything. I'm trying to make some educated guesses and make the appropriate choice to respond. I'm now wondering if this deck shouldn't abandon ship while there is still time."

"They'll destroy the pods." His tone was colored with despair.

"If they have anyone left on their ship to do it, they will," she agreed. "But they may all be on board except for a skeleton crew, and if so can't watch all the ejection points. Hard to weigh the odds because we can't be sure they are really pirates."

"Who else?" Yuri blanched. She knew he was thinking again about the possibilities. Being captured and sold as a slave and worked hard was one thing. There was always the chance of escape or a decent life. His next statement confirmed her supposition that he wasn't thinking positive. "What if it's the Juxtant?"

"The Juxtant are scattered," she dismissed, willing another surge of bile back down. "The Home World and its allies dealt with them, and the Shadalla are cleaning up the dregs."

"We can hope that's all true," he muttered. "At least the Shadalla treats slaves well, and sometimes they ransom—"

"The Shadalla don't buy slaves anymore, Yuri."

"So the treaty says," he agreed, but with true Russian pessimism.

A *thud* signaled the arrival of the lift, cutting Yuri off before she could remind him he was lucky he didn't possess a vagina. As far as she knew, the Shadalla were primarily heterosexual, although that was but a fleeting tidbit of information she'd recalled. An understanding of the sexual proclivities of other species hadn't mattered back then. But now...the majority of the passengers on the ship were female, and it was a damn good possibility someone had told the pirates that very thing. She knew there were species who'd prefer Yuri. A particularly nasty flash surged up from the guarded recesses in that dark room in her brain, battered itself into oblivion, and she blinked back into the present once again. *Breathe. Attend to your surroundings.*

She'd boarded this fucking ship to avoid all the triggers, choosing civilian life after her discharge, and this was so unfair—like life was fair. Neira felt her lip curl at her pathetic musing. Best to get on with it.

The dual panels of the lift shuddered but didn't part company as she motioned Yuri into position on the far side of the conveyance. She supposed the doors were affected by the same issues as the ones to the passenger quarters. A tiny slit manifested in the middle as the business end of a blade poked through the joint. Neira moved swiftly, bringing up her *palka*, and slammed the blade back into the recesses of the door. She distinctly heard a foul curse hard on the heels of her action.

"What do you think they'll do next?" Yuri spoke

in a hushed tone.

"If I was on the other side of the door I'd try a couple of blades at once and hope whoever beat back the first attempt is alone, or got lucky." She ran a finger down her weapon, relieved that there wasn't a mark.

Her only supporter tried a smile, totally at odds with the look of terror in his pale blue eyes. "I'll do my best."

"All I can ask, Yuri," she reassured him, blessing the faulty mechanics that were the only thing standing between them and some very real nastiness. She didn't tell Yuri that repairs might already be underway, in which case the lift doors would fly open and they'd be overwhelmed in an instant, because she'd never be able to hold back a concerted attack by herself. And pirates weren't stupid; they existed in space where others couldn't, so they'd developed a way of surviving she couldn't pretend to understand. Lots of things she didn't understand on this trip. Like why she was really here. What had she been thinking? *And should you have stayed on the Home World? Let them find a way to bring you back into the fold?*

"Are you a soldier?"

Glancing at Yuri, she nodded, wondering if he'd somehow read her mind. "Was. Not for a few months now."

"You quit? Do they allow that?"

"It's called a discharge, my friend, and yes, one can quit." *Not the way you quit, though.* She gave her head a quick shake to shove that thought away and kept her attention on the doors.

"You look like a soldier still. You're fit in ways different than the farmers and the others. And your hair…"

She involuntarily passed a hand over her closely

shorn locks, so unlike the majority of the other women aboard—and some of the men. Her hair had grown out a little since she was discharged and she'd tried to leave it alone, tried to be more feminine, but old habits die hard. *People die hard too, don't they?* Fuck. She couldn't let herself think about this crap now.

"It's easier to care for," she said, wondering why she even bothered to assuage Yuri's curiosity, except maybe their dialogue would keep him calm and up to the task.

"The sonic shower is something less than desirable," he agreed, chatting desultorily. Anxiety was apparent in his stance, and his voice echoed down the long corridor. "There's actual water in showers on some ships. Better recycling or something."

Their only warning was the slice of steel against steel as the two blades Neira had forecast pushed through the narrow crevice of the lift doors. It snapped them both out of their superficial conversation and she mentally cursed her lack of focus. Stepping up, she successfully whacked one back inside, and a crack beside her, accompanied by a muttered profanity, dealt with the other. Yuri blinked her way and the closet support, now in bad repair, dangled from one hand.

"Good job." Her troops wouldn't require praise, but he looked overwhelmed.

"Uh, thanks. I imagined it was a predator coming close to the barns."

Not such a bad analogy, Neira thought, as she considered his now useless weapon. The substance it was made from was no match for tempered steel. "You'll need another rod. You might want to hurry."

Watching him hustle back to his quarters while she waited for the next foray chiseled away at her equanimity. She sucked in a deep breath and exhaled fully. When their attackers came through those doors, barring the miraculous arrival of the Outriders, she'd acquit herself to the best of her ability…and die trying. A calm resolve overtook her and she prepared. This was what she'd been seeking, if only she had admitted it. Not some stifling half-life on a planet nobody else wanted, but death in battle. Guarding the innocent, even if she wouldn't be able to save them either.

Chapter Two

Vayne Palldyn bent a look on his executive officer. "Why is this taking so long?"

Leric Hastel lifted a shoulder and barked a question into his mouthpiece, wincing when a retort clearly filled his ear. He fished the earbud out and turned to Vayne. "They've secured the bridge, the crew quarters and the first deck of passengers. And of course the cargo hold. Some problem on gaining access to the second deck."

"Explain."

"I can't, sir. They won't say. They're clearly agitated."

That wouldn't do. Vayne knew the second deck held primarily women, the soft, curvy women of that Home World—Earth—he'd had cause to visit after the conflict. After his kind and the humans became allies. The place he was no longer welcome to call upon, despite the détente, because someone had figured out he had ulterior motives, someone with a guilty conscience. He'd been lucky to receive forewarning in order to leave a few stints ahead of the assassination teams. The ambassador's daughter had foolishly believed he was committed to her and passed on the message her father had received. No doubt she now wished him ill, considering he hadn't contacted her again as promised, but she wasn't a chosen. In truth it had pained him to use the girl, but she'd been a means to a very essential end. If only he'd had more time. And it wasn't as if he hadn't brought her intense pleasure.

Now here he was, breaking every kind of rule. If not for his position on his own planet, this action could get him executed. If he was found out it would still create some issues, maybe even a scandal. And while his information stated the *Astris* carried a large female passenger contingent, he had no idea of the age of said females, yet decided to take the risk. He was that desperate. His species was that desperate, the treaty and all its old, doddering males who supported it, be damned. "We should have taken the *Astris* ourselves."

"No, sir. The pirates seizing her gives you plausible deniability."

Vayne snorted a laugh despite the circumstances. His exec had adopted several interesting political sayings from their previous enemy and used them well. "This is true, Leric. But you've already said there was a phase weapon discharged. Who is to say they won't completely fuck up the remainder of the mission? I hope to find an appropriate mate in one of those women."

"I understand that. But you can't think to go over there."

He cogitated. His ship, *Tomodr*, stood off from the pirates' battered one, using the profile to screen it from any possible detection by the *Astris* in the event someone on that bridge had detected the attack coming. He knew the Outriders would soon be on their way back, because their slower charge had been at a standstill long enough for the security ships to have lost the old style ion beacon. He decided.

"I'm going. You have the con. Send two troops with me."

"Sir!" It was Leric's job as first officer to protest, but he would know the futility in it as he knew his sovereign. Vayne wouldn't change his mind, not with his possible prey—*some* Shadalla male's prey—so close.

"Tell those fools to cease whatever they are doing to attempt to take that deck! And tell them not to kill anyone else." Surely everyone worthy of being an opponent was now subdued. It was a *passenger* ship, for fuck's sake.

At Leric's resigned acceptance, Vayne made his way to the lift, relieving another officer of his weapon as he did so, the shocker being far less dangerous in closed quarters than a fucking phase weapon. Assholes.

The two troopers he'd ordered joined him at the shuttle, and a pilot was already at the controls. Vayne decided to let the smaller man fly her. He was an excellent pilot himself, but he wanted to concentrate on the more immediate—getting this mission *done*. They gained the docking port on the beleaguered ship in a few moments, and upon entering the bay he surveyed the motley human pirates milling about as they alternately cursed and glared his way.

"Captain?" He afforded their leader the respect the pirate probably didn't deserve, but it accomplished what he required. The other man—previously seen only on vids—stepped forward and gave Vayne his attention.

"There was no need to attend, Sovereign. None." The captain spoke quietly but with intent.

Vayne's gut clenched. The pirate had figured out who he really was, despite using false names and considerable currency to blur the reasoning. He rose above it, ignoring the title. "Explain the problem."

With a faint sneer, Captain Ristos gestured toward the corridor. "Come."

Leaving everyone behind except for his troops, who'd fanned out to protect his flank, Vayne followed Ristos. Assorted *Astris* crew members wearing the distinguished green-and-gold uniforms of the transport line were tied up and stacked against the walls, and all were blindfolded. At least his orders not to use ultimate force had been followed. Ristos came to a halt and gestured. Vayne noted how well made the other man was, tall and muscular, and he'd clearly seen the inside of a sonic shower recently. A quick glance around determined the remainder of the pirates were also well set up and tidy about their persons despite their mismatched appearances and frustrated demeanor. It struck him he was dealing with something quite different from that of the killers and marauders he expected.

"It's the same on the bridge. We killed no one. The captain refused to tell the crew to stand down, so he was…made an example, and the rest followed suit for the most part. Stunned several, beat a few into submission, but we have control."

Surveying Ristos with new interest, Vayne saw what the vids hadn't shown him—the man was intelligent and obviously a leader of men. That much was evident in the deportment of the ones who followed him. Perhaps some kind of disbanded military? "You don't have control of the second deck."

"Yet," the other man agreed grimly. "We thought it was a mechanical problem. The gravitational systems were damaged by an overenthusiastic crew who thought he was releasing the fucking docking clamps and dissuading us. It's made every door on the ship either slow to open or, in the case of the lift, impossible. Then some fool used a phase weapon and destroyed the back-up systems."

Vayne waited, and Ristos' black eyes narrowed as he explained in detail. "We thought the second deck lift doors were also merely stuck, needed a manual push. But the man I had prying it open insists both his blade, and that of his comrade, were pushed back on them. It's a ridiculous stand-off, and we don't know who is on the other side."

"I apologize for thinking you less than professional," Vayne offered.

"Well, don't praise me yet, Sovereign. We lost a

pod too. One passenger, female, probably a passenger and unlikely to be skilled at avoidance, but there's still a risk—"

"Of the Home World getting a transmission, even via an outpost or another ship," Vayne concluded.

"Your part in this won't likely be in that report, but it does mean we need to get moving and retrieve that pod. And so far we haven't been able to repair those damn doors!"

"Are you suggesting we cut our losses?" That was most definitely not happening, and Vayne's tone reflected the fact.

Ristos shrugged. "We got the cargo, what there was of it. The Home World isn't sending as much out to its colonies anymore. I expect they're self-sufficient. More tends to come back. For import, as it were. But they like to make their stamp on whatever they touch."

Vayne wasn't going to respond to that resonating comment, because he'd likely lose his temper and destroy a few things, waste too much time. Would he ever move past the rage? "What was the number of males to females in the first deck?"

He was determined to hide his real reason for waylaying the *Astris*, though Ristos clearly wasn't stupid. He also regretted the severe injury to the Home World captain and made a mental note to find out who the man's family was and ensure they wanted for nothing in the event the man wasn't able to work again. Vayne hated only the politicians, and those high up in Earth's military, the ones who gave the orders...and collaborated with his worst enemy.

"Fifty-two females, sixteen males." He yanked his thoughts away from the Juxtant Monarch as Ristos supplied the information.

"And their stats?"

"All females well above forty, sent to oversee or work in the installations on Vector Seven. Skilled. I suspect they are going because there is nothing left for them at home. The men are all in their prime, farm labor."

"Are the men willing to work for better wages and conditions?" Vayne made another effort to mask his real intent.

The other man shrugged. "None agreed. They think it's a trick. I do suspect that if they thought we'd kill them they'd take the deal."

"We want those willing to move. We aren't interested in guarding people who will try to run, or worse, sabotage our facilities." Vayne heard himself confiding in a pirate captain and wished to call back the words. Except the man somehow was felt to be his equal, if not in birthright, then as a warrior. It was puzzling and something he needed to consider at a later date. His species didn't tend to play well with others.

"Uh-huh. And the women are too old? Well, then I suggest we leave them locked in their quarters. Second deck will likely yield the same results. We've downloaded the computer files but they're encrypted. So we don't know everything, yet." The pirate leader's features gave away nothing but Vayne felt his thoughts and silent queries. The sovereign knew there were women on board, as he was privy to the manifest, and females of childbearing age were worth this risk.

Forcing a casual gesture, Vayne said quietly, "Best not look too closely, my friend. Speculation can be dangerous."

Ristos regarded him with interest—and no real fear. It took Vayne aback. His threat had been unmistakable for such an intelligent man to discount it. "I don't care what your game is, Sovereign, although I suspect it isn't just about manning your facilities. If you want access to that deck, then you'll have it."

Accompanying the pirate captain, Vayne approached the lift. It was sizable but would hardly hold an assault force. Ristos clearly had the same opinion, motioning out the four pirates already there before heading in himself. He looked at Vayne, one brow raised in invitation, and Vayne stepped inside.

"Barek and Duff, you come with us. Want one of your troops, sir?"

Aware Ristos had deliberately not afforded him his title, now that others were within earshot, Vayne shook his head and ignored the look of concern on his guards' faces. "Stand down. Aid in the clean-up and any transfers."

The doors hitched closed on their startled faces and his stomach dropped as they fell to the lower deck, the *whooshing* sound of the lift very apparent in the silence. He sincerely hoped the difficulty with the systems didn't extend to the conveyance, because being stuck like a *lorat* in a cage didn't appeal. Nor did ending up as a broken bundle of flesh should it free fall. When it stopped without incident at its appropriate destination, he turned to the captain, hiding his sigh of relief. "Your plan?"

"Same as before, only with three blades. Whoever is on the other side can't defend forever with whatever weapons they have. And with any luck my tech officer will have the repairs made shortly. If it wasn't for that escape pod I'd counsel we wait."

Standing back, Vayne observed as Ristos and his men inserted their long daggers into the crack between the doors simultaneously and began to pry from opposite directions. The pirate called Barek was a great hulk of a man, and he grunted loudly as his efforts offset the other two. Then he and Ristos staggered back, blades vibrating visibly in their hands. Duff almost immediately took one step back, but his blade didn't leave the door completely. He resumed prying, but his weapon visibly shuddered, and he too retreated.

Curses filled the air, and Ristos turned a wry smile on Vayne. "It appears we have determined opponents, sir."

Daggers at the ready, the three once again approached the crack when there was a mechanical sigh and the doors opened. Vayne spied a young, fair-haired male standing wide-eyed, his mouth dropping open as the pirates charged from the lift. Vayne followed on their heels, wincing as they mowed the young man down with a hit to the head, the impact throwing him into the corridor wall. Then all chaos descended.

A significantly smaller figure, dressed completely in black, waded into the triangle of pirates. It laid Barek low with well-placed blows to his knees and an uppercut to his jaw as he fell to the ground. The baton inflicting the punishment flashed in a blur of movement to match the warrior's whirling grace. Vayne was already moving to assist when the fighting dervish dealt with Duff, body moving with grace and deadly intent, bringing the pirate down with punishment to his kidneys. Short black hair gleamed in the harsh lighting as the warrior spun to take on Ristos, who'd become tangled in Barek's long arms as he sprawled, almost senseless.

Vayne used his shocker, nearly catching one slender, black clad shoulder as their opponent made contact with Ristos' ribcage, the baton making a dull, wet sound in contrast with the captain's growl of pain and rage. But the little warrior whirled out of range, turning to renew the attack, and the bolt spent itself harmlessly against the bulkhead. Vayne's cock filled and stood at full attention, causing him considerable discomfort in his tight-fitting space uniform. By the shades of Turco, it was a female. And what a female. He locked eyes with orbs a brilliant shade of the golden gemstones so prized on his planet before she charged, moving gracefully on the balls of her bare feet.

"He dies!" Duff's howl cut through the tension as Vayne prepared to defend himself, and the female halted, stumbling as she did so. Duff held his weapon at the young male's throat, vicious intent written across his features.

"No, don't," the lithe beauty called out, and Vayne watched, transfixed, as she dropped to her knees, carefully laying down the lethal weapon she used so efficiently. She then clasped her hands behind her neck. Her voice, while plaintive and breathless, was nearly musical to his ears.

Nothing in her posture spoke of true submission, but it didn't matter to Vayne's cock. That appendage throbbed painfully and he was at a loss as to how to calm it. Never had he ever… Vayne struggled to make his body move. Captain Ristos moved first.

Kicking aside the baton, he gestured to Duff, who released his hold on the still-unconscious young male and pulled his dagger away. Was this woman attached to the man? Guarding him? Vayne shook his head. It didn't matter.

"Secure her."

Ristos bent and clipped a pair of solar cuffs around the woman's wrists, and Vayne approved of how efficient the captain was, yet afforded the little female respect. He wasn't the only male to appreciate her attempt to defend this deck. The restraints emitted slight *whirring* sounds as they engaged. Charged by any light source, they were virtually impervious to tampering and would open only to the owner's print. Vayne pulled the control from the captain's hand, entered his own print to replace Ristos', then crushed the control beneath his boot. The pirate captain didn't blink an eye, though his two men exhibited some slight surprise.

"Help one another to our ship," Ristos instructed them. He waited as they hobbled to the lift, throwing glances of retribution mixed with awe toward the woman still kneeling in the corridor.

"I'll bring the other passengers out and offer them your conditions, Sov—sir."

Vayne gave up any pretense. As desperate as the Shadalla were, their scientists had confirmed the compatibility of Earth females to breed and bear their children, and some of his species' males had actually found their chosen. Gone was Vayne's need to merely pick a female out of the women on this ship, using careful parameters to ensure she was suited for his position, able to bear his children, and of a nature and appearance to stimulate his desires in order to put those offspring in her belly. Royal concubines weren't unheard of, after all, and the odds of him finding a chosen were slight. But he couldn't look any further, impossibly drawn to this imperious warrior at his feet. And should he ever be fortunate enough to find an actual chosen mate, this lovely woman would retain concubine status, regardless.

"Bring the men out. Offer. I'll send my exec to scrutinize the females." He wasn't that overwhelmed to forget he had a duty to other men in his service, Leric included.

"Good. And then we're off. A pod to recover. And if you require any other...services..."

"And if *you* require anything I might be able to provide. Any assistance?" Vayne offered.

"I might take you up on that someday, sir."

Nodding, he reached down and fit a hand under

the elbow of the female, and his world turned upside down. The physical attraction had been immediate, granted. But the instant he touched her and her scent enveloped him, his brain exploded with a revelation he'd only experienced once in his life—and a very subdued and pale version at that, one manipulated by science. Vayne didn't need another minute with her to understand the symptoms and wished to shout his joy out loud. *She was a chosen* and not his future concubine. She came up with the lightness of gossamer, and only his quick reflexes saved him from a knee to the groin as he turned to catch the blow on his thigh. Little spitfire.

Ristos assisted him, binding her feet with yet another pair of solar cuffs, this time passing the control over without a pause. "She'll use her teeth too," the man commented.

He didn't want to gag her but accepted the inevitable. Still reeling from the fortuitous news, he nodded and strove to recover his equilibrium. Watching as the captain wrapped a silk sash around her mouth, he wrestled with the need to punch the other man in the face for touching her. Vayne also wished he'd asked her name before she was silenced, but he was ruefully aware she'd likely deny him.

She went over his shoulder, body radiating fury, and he blessed the makeshift gag. He was tempted to smack her curved bottom but thought she'd struggle and end up harming herself against the unforgiving walls. There was time enough ahead to gentle his wee warrior.

"Hand me the baton," he requested. "She seems to have an attachment to it."

Ristos scooped it up, running a hand down its gleaming length. "It's a well-crafted and balanced tool. She could have killed with it."

But she hadn't, and Vayne thought he already had

some insight into his as yet nameless bride. Ristos had likely noticed too, hence his care in cuffing her. Control was Vayne's own watchword and this woman also possessed it. It was perhaps unfortunate she would be required to concede that quality, but such was the way of his people.

"Thank you, Captain. I wish you the best. Perhaps we'll cross paths in the future."

The lift bore them up to the docking bay in good time and he stepped out, ignoring the attention he drew. His troops, looking relieved then surprised, fell in behind him as he found the way to the shuttle. He deposited his slight burden on the nearest seating and buckled her in. The glow in those remarkable eyes should have singed him, and on impulse he tugged the gag from her lips.

"What is your name, little warrior?" He spoke in Earth's primary language. He and Ristos had used a different form of communication to safeguard their covert operation, one agreed upon when he'd first contracted with the pirate.

"Fuck you, asshole." The universal translator embedded in his cranium had no difficulty in translating her response. He didn't require it in this case, considering his ability to learn various languages for his time spent on the Home World.

Her epithet was nothing less than he expected. He smiled at her and was rewarded with a flicker of shock. Perhaps she'd expected a cuff or a punch? He would never abuse her, but they would need to discuss how she tempted fate with casual disregard for her circumstances. There were many who would have taken advantage of her helplessness following such a response, maybe broken her lips or blackened an eye in retaliation.

"You'll be somewhat uncomfortable for a short while, my nameless warrior, but after witnessing your abilities I won't remove your restraints until I get you on my own ship."

"You're Shadalla." There was now nothing but calm observation in her tone, all fury abruptly extinguished.

"I am." On impulse, he spoke in his own tongue.

"We have a treaty." She too had a device to translate their conversation. Interesting. He hadn't expected the passengers on the *Astris* to be so equipped.

"We do."

"But you attacked, ignored it."

Vayne bowed his head, a slight move to acknowledge her accusation. "There is a good reason, little one. As you will come to learn."

"Coward. You prey on the weak and defenseless."

The dig struck home, but he schooled his features. "Perhaps you will also come to reconsider in time."

"What do you want with me?"

He saw no fear in those eyes, nothing to intimate she feared for her life, but rather, something he didn't want to interpret. He realized she was not averse to dying and he recoiled, horrified. He intuited her thoughts. This woman was weary to the bone behind her determined efforts to repel the boarders. Those efforts indeed hadn't been in defense of her life but rather of her fellow passengers. She hadn't been attempting to kill the pirates but take them out of commission, at great risk to herself. Courting death. What had brought her to this state? To cover his revelation, he asked a question instead of answering hers.

"Who was that young male to you?" It was an effort not to hold his breath while she answered.

"Who? Yuri? He's a fellow traveler."

Relieved he hadn't taken her from her mate, even if he'd have done so had that been true, Vayne shook his

31

head at her description. "You are no ordinary traveler. You have an embedded universal translator. And you fought like no passenger destined for the outer planets."

Her eyes shuttered and she withdrew from him. He literally watched her go and tried to draw her back, a hint of panic chiseling away at his determination. "Little warrior? Who are you?"

"Who are you?" she countered after a long pause, her eyes coming back into focus.

"Lord Vayne Palldyn, Sovereign of the Southern Range, planet Nibiru. Shadalla." He gave his title proudly, having been granted it through circumstances more than his birth. No royal assumed the throne without proving himself, usually with great sacrifice, and he was no exception. He'd lost both his father and mother, as well as his only sibling as a result of his ambition. There were times when he regretted seeking such status despite his family's approval, because assassins weren't picky about collateral damage. Jostling for the position of sovereign had all but vanished over the decades, and Vayne hoped it was primarily because of his ability to rule and their planet to prosper.

"Holy shit. His Lordship himself," she muttered, and he forgot to think of that sad and violent past.

"You know of me?" Part of him was pleased, another, worried. How could this scrap of womanhood know of him as His Lordship, unless she was indeed military? Then again, the Home World politicians had spies everywhere.

She didn't answer, and he accepted the mystery. For now. They needed to get gone, to quote the pirate captain. He gave the order, settling into a seat beside his nameless prize, and secured his belts. The scanner on his vessel would pick up any devices she might have been implanted with, and he could manage one slender female.

It wasn't like she was going anywhere other than to Nibiru.

They gained the *Tomodr* without incident and he again carried her on board, sensibly replacing the silk sash across her full mouth. Her eyes spit retribution and he longed to make her his. Longed to take her beneath him to instruct her in his need and dominance, while bringing her the utmost pleasure. But it was far too early, and he had many other tools in his repertoire to improve her attitude. Their joining must be with her consent. She would wish it with everything she had. He'd see to it.

Leric was already away on another shuttle to carry out his orders, and Vayne hoped his exec was as fortunate as he. Carrying his future down the corridor to his quarters, he calculated the time back to Nibiru and chose the long route, stopping only to key it in on the com for his navigator.

"Sir."

He spun around to face the crewman, his female shifting on his shoulder as he did so. He felt the strength ripple in her belly muscles as she adjusted and Vayne became impossibly aroused, making him snap at his subordinate. "What is it?"

"The Outriders have reversed their flight pattern."

"How soon?"

"We have perhaps fifteen stints for anonymous departure. No more."

"Recall Leric in ten and be prepared to leap to starblaze. No delays."

"Yes, sir." The man hustled away in the direction of the bridge and Vayne was able to gain his quarters without additional interruptions.

Applying his hand to the sensor pad, he waited impatiently as the panel opened in response, then carried his warrior in.

After lowering her to his bunk—even sovereigns didn't rate luxuries on a warship—Vayne knelt beside her and gently tugged the silk free. She'd been restrained long enough.

"I'm going to release you on your promise you won't attempt to escape or otherwise act out."

"No chance." Those golden eyes gave no quarter, and her wide mouth, with its shorter upper lip, curled in disdain. He wanted to lick it back into its sweet curve but valued his own flesh.

"We're in the middle of no man's space, little one. No place to run, nowhere to hide."

"Then you have nothing to worry about."

With a sigh, and an eye on his timepiece, he released her wrists first. He took advantage of her obvious stiffness to snatch one hand, replace the cuff and attach it to a bolt on the headboard. She flexed her free hand and eyed the bolt—and the matching one on the other side. A faint flush covered her high cheekbones.

"You're a pervert, too." The statement was curiously without affect.

"You have no idea," he agreed amiably. If his little captive recognized the symbolism of the bolts, then she might not require the immersion in his culture he'd expected during the holding period. He was both titillated at the thought and disappointed, having hoped to be the first to introduce her to the pleasure of bondage while being pleasured to madness. Another look at her face doused both emotions. Resignation dulled her eyes for an instant, even as she quickly blinked it away. The impression of something terrible rolled over him but he shoved his prescience down for the moment. He had to get his ship out of range before he allowed himself to begin to share her emotions. Her death wish had already colored his mind, and the reasons behind such a thing would likely be dire.

With a press of his digit on the cuffs at her ankles, her feet came free and he took himself out of kicking distance.

"I'll come back with sustenance when I'm able," he advised.

"Don't rush on my part." He thought she also called him a name under her breath as he left his quarters, ensuring the door locked securely behind him, and made his way to the bridge. He paused near the shuttle bay.

"Sir." Leric panted, and behind him Vayne saw several figures sporting long, flowing hair being shepherded into extra crew quarters. Three troops were hard on their heels, along with his medic.

"How many?"

"Twelve females. All lovely specimens. The men refused our offer." Leric didn't need to add that there had been no offer made to the females. If they were of age, thought capable of bearing children and appeared healthy, they had been taken. There had been no time for the medic to ascertain their suitability on the *Astris*.

"And for you? Were you blessed?"

"There is a fair-haired female with enormous brown eyes. She is very frightened, and I had to tamp down my desperation, but I touched her and sensed…" His exec, never at a loss for words, faltered. Vayne smiled and thumped the other man's arm.

"Then go with your instinct, my friend. If she occupies your thoughts and you crave her more than food and drink, she is a chosen. And she will never find a kinder man, despite our need for dominance. Or a more deserving one."

"My thanks, Sovereign." Leric visibly brought himself under control, his shoulders squaring and his head once again raised, eyes alert. "Orders?"

"Go. Put as much space between us and the *Astris* as possible. I've alerted the navigator of the route to take a different path home, something to both confuse any pursuit and give us some time to woo our future brides." Though in truth his little warrior was already essentially bound to him, as was Leric's choice of a lifemate.

"Do you believe the Home World will send others to try and follow?"

"I don't, because there's no reason for them to think we were involved. The pirates will have left some sort of decoy, as well. But this entire operation has taken too long, and I won't risk anything. We move now."

"Yes, sir. Done."

Vayne supervised their departure and allowed a sigh of relief when they left the *Astris* behind. The pirate ship was also departing. The only thing for the Outriders to find would be the drifting passenger vessel, with its entire crew essentially unharmed and most of its passengers still on board. The loss of thirteen female travelers would no doubt be investigated, but with pirates involved, it was likely the authorities would accept that loss. Women weren't as valued on the Home World as they should be, and losing the paltry cargo would probably make a greater impact.

If he'd really wanted to muddy the trail Vayne would have ordered everyone on board slaughtered, and there had been a time in Shadalla history when that would have been the case. But he'd seen too much violence and perpetrated too much. Now that the war was over he had no taste for duty in the form of dealing death, although there were some remaining humans who would find it at his hand when they were ferreted out. But that was a process he'd set in motion with others more skilled in the hunt, having missed his opportunity. And he now had other, more important, things on his mind. One in particular.

Instructing a crew member in the galley as to the contents of a tray he was required to formulate, Vayne leaned against the bulkhead. Fatigue, more from the emotional stress of the day, wore at him. Accepting the tray, he wearily trudged back to his quarters, sustenance in hand. The scent of the food lifted his tiredness to some extent and he stared down at the meal. It had been a long journey and a momentous one. Some time had passed since he'd flown a ship on a mission. Politics had taken up far too much of his time. It was a tasteless, if necessary, task.

As he neared his cabin, he could sense her and she was like a stimulant. He forgot any weariness as it washed away before his sense of anticipation and he commanded the door to open. His little warrior was where he'd left her, ensconced on his bunk, the disheveled bedding indicative of how she'd attempted to break free. Vayne actually entered with caution, insanely thinking she might have escaped her binds and was waiting on the other side of the panel to wreak havoc. On him. The anticipation of warring with his bride, and the resulting loving reparations, nearly consumed him. His cock, still tumescent, expressed its agreement.

She watched him warily, like a wild *leicat*, those animals now few and far between on his planet. His people's efforts at conservation had been too late for many of their native species, though they had a better track record than some other worlds. Like his little warrior's Home World. Vayne set his jaw at the thoughts of the things he'd witnessed there. Barbarians, and obviously as capable of genocide as the Juxtant. Certainly more effective in delivering it.

Her breathing was measured and she appeared in complete control, and Vayne again wondered who she was, then became determined to find out. Before she became his and her past was obscured and lost, as was necessary. No one would find her and it would be as if she never existed elsewhere.

"I have food and drink. Will you tell me your name?"

"Do I get fed if I refuse?"

"Of course. I have no interest in harming you. I merely thought you might want to hold on to some of yourself. Share your name and I will not assign you another."

With a short intake of breath, she stared at him, those interesting eyes sharp and shimmering with intelligence. "Explain."

"You are mine, little warrior. For eternity. How you accept that will be your choice, but I never lose, and in this I cannot afford to lose. You will come to understand."

"So you've said. Maybe try and explain now."

He hesitated, then put most of the information out there for her. Perhaps if she understood what the Shadalla were facing… "We are in dire need of childbearing mates. The majority of our women are sterile because of your Home World's genetic weapons. And many died from the resulting infections until our scientists could determine the cause. By then it was too late. We males outnumber our females by thousands to one and we are not a proliferate species."

"What?" Shock and disbelief were embodied in that one word.

"Which part shocks you, little one? What part don't you believe? We are uncomfortable allies, your kind and mine, and most recently only because of our desire to unite to battle the Juxtant. But before that, your people's insidious weapon was somehow carried home from the war and infiltrated our world. We had no awareness of it until perhaps a decade ago and even then could barely attribute it to the ones who rule your planet. We thought them better than the Juxtant." Until he'd come into the information about collusion, something that never left his mind.

"I'm not shocked about the genetic weapon. I believe you," she said, her tone so bitter and dark it took him aback. "The Home World is ruled by greedy cowards."

Her obvious hatred of her own leaders might help his case, and Vayne made a mental note. He then considered it was his assertion that he'd taken her to be his lifemate that caused such shock. Unfortunate, but not surprising. He thought she might say more, then realized she once again retreated into her own thoughts. That would never do when they were joined, and he added it to the mental list of things he must teach her.

Combining a few pieces of fruit and cheese on a plate, then adding dried meat and bread, he carried it over and set it on the small table beside the bunk, watching the entire time for any indication she might use her feet against him. Returning to take a chair and dole out food for himself, he studied her.

"You believe me, and aren't shocked because you served those same authorities?" he suggested.

Her face immediately tightened and her eyes became more remote. She didn't answer, so he continued. "We don't choose to die out as a race, so we've found another way."

"You kidnap Home World women and breed them." The bald statement fell between them. So much for avoidance.

"Not quite so…cold. Or callous."

"Really." She shifted on his bunk, ignoring the

food. "What would you call it? Although I can understand the need for revenge, considering how heinous their act."

"It's not revenge. I do allow it might be viewed as such by women like yourself." He paused at her snort.

"You've never kidnapped anyone like me, mister."

"I know that to be true, and I consider myself blessed, little warrior." His voice thrummed with the depth of his emotion.

"What? Why?" There was agitation evident in *her* voice, and he wondered at it. Could it be she was unmanned by a hint of kindness? Of appreciation?

"I saw how you fought, and I see your intelligence. You are perfect for me. Perfect to carry on my line." If she tested capable of conceiving, he reminded himself, and decided not to share that thought with her. In fact, the very idea of her being infertile made his belly clench. Surely the gods wouldn't be so cruel. But he would have her regardless, as his bride, and find a surrogate to provide his children.

"Not interested."

The flat refusal to accept his edict, with no explanation, no additional protest, irked him. He grabbed at a straw. Perhaps she indeed had a mate on the Home World…and children. Her grief was palpable, if contained, and while he wouldn't return her, perhaps something could be done about the offspring. "Are you married? Do you have children?"

She gave another quick bark of laughter, the harsh sound nearly passing for humor. "No. And no. Not in the cards. Ever."

Ignoring her outburst, he said, "Then I'm relieved you won't be mourning them. It would have made things more difficult, if not insurmountable."

She narrowed her eyes and stared. Despite

himself, the fine hair on the back of his neck prickled and he wondered how many men she had faced down with that look. "So it wouldn't have made a difference, then."

"No. Regrettably, no. I would have made it a priority to locate your children and bring them to you. But the Shadalla are desperate and in the need of lifemates."

"Well, I'm not yours."

He was tired of explaining himself and stating the obvious. "As you noted earlier, you and your fellow female travelers have no choice."

"How many others?"

He found himself answering without thought. "Twelve." This woman was already affecting his ability to dissemble. Truly this was ordained.

"Are they all right? Was anyone hurt?" She tugged against the cuff, obviously agitated.

"Your concern is noteworthy, little one. They are fine. Being fed and cared for. And there will be no breeding. Yet." He couldn't help himself from describing it that way, still smarting from her rejection, while he knew that to be ludicrous, considering he had kidnapped her for that very purpose. It would take time—and persuasion—to help her view things differently. And he needed to manage his male ego better.

Her glare was answer enough.

"Eat something," he urged. This was the last time during the holding period when she would eat by her own hand.

Her tethers were long enough to easily reach the table and she picked at the food, avoiding his gaze. He turned his attention to his own repast, consuming it quickly before pouring them both some *valki*. He set the glass beside her plate, noting that she didn't even spare him a glance. But she didn't use her feet against him, either.

She sat back and regarded him after drinking most of the ale but leaving a good portion of the meal. "So, what now?"

"I won't force you, if that is what you fear."

"I don't fear much of anything," she said flatly.

He believed she thought it to be true, seeing that remote look descend upon her face yet again. If she couldn't resist physically, she'd withdraw emotionally— he knew all too well how that worked. But she hadn't met anyone like him before, and he was already producing pheromones in great quantity. "I'll release you so you can use the facilities, shower if you like. But the outer door is secure and coded. Should you manage to incapacitate me, you'll not leave these quarters."

"And you might never leave them." A flat assertion.

Vayne laughed, although he recognized the truth in her statement. "Then neither would you. My men would be forced to dispatch the woman who killed their sovereign, as much as I'd regret it."

"And then kill the rest of the hostages."

"No, little warrior. That's not how this works. They are innocents. They will be taken care of, placed with men who will cherish them."

She studied him, her golden eyes darkening with some emotion he couldn't interpret. "And bear them mini Shadallas." She raised one slim shoulder. "I'll behave, but only because I require the facilities. Unless you break your promise."

"Never." He wouldn't need to force her. She would come to him and beg for his cock. Not that he would humiliate her when she did so.

He released the cuffs, and time stretched out between them as their proximity heightened the tension.

He scented her, a faint, spicy bouquet overlaid with the clean sweat of her exertions outside that lift and it wove the connection deeper. He could only imagine what touching her would do. His desire for her surged higher at the memory of the way she'd dealt with two enormous villains. She would probably have taken down the captain as well if not for being blackmailed into surrendering. Vayne again reminded himself who he held captive in his quarters. It wouldn't do for his men to find him dispatched.

Stepping back, he motioned to the cleansing area. His bride slipped from the bunk and gracefully passed out of his line of sight. He gathered the remains of their meal onto the tray and set it on a table in the corner before retrieving both cuffs and setting them down for easy access. Then he stripped out of the restricting uniform, releasing his sorely confined cock and blowing out his breath with huge relief. It had been a day for sighing, and he wasn't familiar with the emotion that produced a sigh. For a moment, the memory of Asula etched itself on his forebrain before essentially dissolving and being replaced with that of his little warrior. Vayne didn't know if that was an omen but thought he would take it as such. His deceased wife never had power or importance in his life, regrettably, and now was not the time to spend any thinking of her.

The shower hissed on, and he hustled into the bathing area, snatching up the black clothing and a scrap of fabric he recognized as an undergarment. Dropping them into the cleansing unit, he then relieved himself with some difficulty because of his erection and donned a soft garment to cover his lower body. He watched his lifemate step from the shower chamber.

She was all ivory skin and shadowed hollows, her body as honed as those on his planet who excelled in performance sports. Small, firm breasts sat high on her torso, tipped with tight red buds, and her feminine cleft nestled between long, slender thighs. Tiny droplets of recycled water highlighted every dip and curve. Vayne bit back a groan as his beast begged him to take her, dominate and make her his own.

"Where are my clothes?" Standing without any attempt to cover herself, secure in her own skin, his female stared at him.

"You won't require any in my quarters."

"Bullshit."

"Ah, little one. Your turn of phrase amuses me, though it could become wearing."

Staring at the front of his underpiece, she quirked a brow, not acknowledging his gentle threat. His cock filling again, Vayne struggled with the urge to correct her but gave in to the greater need to laugh. He hadn't been amused in a long time. She appeared startled when he chuckled.

"Go to bed, my warrior."

"Clothes."

"Not necessary. And I already gave you my word."

After another assessing stare, she eased past him. For an instant his eyes closed when pure, raw need overtook him. Almost immediately aware of how vulnerable his lack of sight made him, he blinked wide and looked to see her reach the bunk. She sank down on the edge, and he saw her exhaustion as her shoulders slumped forward, her profile dipping in concert. And he believed it wasn't only from the day's events but from something far deeper and far reaching, like her concealed grief. A startling need to protect her coursed through his veins and he approached the bed.

"Move to the far side, lie back and raise your

hands. I'm going to cuff you and shorten the tethers. I need to rest, and I don't trust you as yet."

"So sleep elsewhere. I prefer not to be tied up."

"This is *my* cabin, little warrior. And we will share quarters from here on in. Move over and raise your hands."

She obeyed him, clearly having weighed the alternatives, but her anger simmered, tangible and cloying. He restrained her wrists and hooked a length of silken rope to one of the bolts, leaving enough slack for her to roll over and also partially lower her arms to allow blood flow, but not enough to allow her to cause him bodily harm while he slept. He didn't care to be garroted. How he'd actually sleep was anyone's guess, when his balls ached as though he hadn't emptied them for *gordis*.

She was so lovely, with her round breasts lifted as if for his touch, the long line of her waist and slight swell of her hips drawing him in. The thin strip of dark curls on her mound was in direct contrast to the smoothness of her labia, and he longed to open her there and trace her inner petals, search out her nub of pleasure and find her opening. He yearned to fuck her and wondered how he'd ever restrain himself until the holding period was over. His beast paced within. For the first time, Vayne cursed his culture but allowed it was steeped not only in tradition but in solid common sense. The Shadalla had kidnapped females in the distant past, and the rules put in place then held considerable practicality today. It was why they'd turned to them again—with human females.

"Are you comfortable?"

"Fine." She bit off the word and looked away.

"Slide farther over, my little warrior."

With a huff, she did as he instructed, nearly to the wall, breasts bobbling enticingly. She then turned onto her side, giving him the length of her back. His own breath caught as he viewed what he'd missed earlier—the scarring of her skin, thin welts placed precisely, one beneath the other, from her shoulders to the small of her back. Squinting, he could see fainter marks on the fullness of her buttocks and upper thighs. Clearly, the additional tissue there had healed more easily than the thinner skin of her back. She had been whipped countless times, and perhaps her flesh hadn't healed between the assaults, the ridged lines as exact as if drawn by a straight edge. The fine line of skin between each of them was a mockery of what had likely been as beautiful as the front of her.

Vayne wrestled with such a surge of rage his temples pounded and the breath stuttered in his chest. He opened his mouth to ask her what happened, then shut it tightly. The markings may well have been consensual. Many cultures practiced such things, humans among them. There was much to learn about his intended.

She rolled her head slightly and caught him staring, perhaps had felt the heat of his gaze. "I told you I recognized perverts. Your Lordship."

He reared back and sought the words, any words, for she'd confirmed his darkest thoughts. He reached out and touched his fingertips to her back, tracing the welts, feeling the silken skin between the scars ripple as she shuddered away. Perhaps he was wrong, and he had to know. "Did you ask for this? Want this?" It was better than the alternative.

"Fuck you, Sovereign. You get no more from me."

She looked toward the wall as he brought his reaction under control. There would be time tomorrow to address her withholding. The process of integration had already begun. He could feel it, unable to think of anyone but her, the empty place in him eagerly preparing to be filled and completed. He climbed into the bunk beside her, aware of its width, or lack of it, and relished the closeness. She wouldn't be able to hide from him for long.

"Sleep well, my little warrior. We have much to discuss and explore on the morrow."

He instructed the computer to dim the lights and darkness crept over the room.

"My name is Neira. Don't call me little one, little warrior, or anything else. I don't like it and you're not entitled."

Smiling into the dark, he shifted and fit against the back of Neira's body, ignoring how she immediately tensed. Neira. He tasted it. *Neira*. But she'd always be his little warrior, and perhaps one day she would come to ask him to call her as such.

In time she relaxed, incrementally, and when he was satisfied she was asleep, Vayne allowed himself to slip into slumber.

Chapter Three

Neira came awake like the soldier she'd been—sleep to total awareness. She woke from a dead sleep, though, not from that curious near-wakeful state she shared with most of her comrades-in-arms both on and off the fields of battle. So that meant her subconscious had reason to believe she'd fallen asleep in a place of safety.

But that didn't fit with the fact her hands were tethered, or with the immediate surge of memory relaying the events of the following day. It certainly didn't fit with the presence of a large, heated body spooning her, a very definite poke of a solid erection in the small of her back. She was in her captor's bed, without even the slight barrier or protection of night clothes. She thought he'd worn some kind of undergarment...

"You are awake." A face nuzzled her hair and a mouth pressed a kiss on her temple.

Neira flirted with the thought of flipping over and setting her teeth in the flesh of that handsome face while bringing her knee up into that hard appendage. Instead, she inched away from his attentions, continuing to give him her back. If she thought she might manage to get his print on the release of her cuffs, she'd have tried it, but the sovereign was a big bugger, and he moved well. The scar on his chest wasn't from some weird rite of passage, but from a knife with a big, serrated blade. She well knew the pattern of injury, having seen a fair number over the years. That meant Vayne Palldyn was also a warrior, not that she hadn't heard the stories of his military prowess. It was unlikely she'd get the drop on him.

He'd somehow missed her dagger in the commotion, and she'd secreted it in the wash facility upon working it free from under her tunic. She hoped there'd be an opportunity to use it and gain her freedom and refused to listen to the practical voice in her head that asked how she thought she might accomplish that task. She had planned to retrieve it after her cleansing, take it to the bed to hide it there and protect herself but was foiled by Palldyn's presence in the room. And it turned out she hadn't needed it after all. He'd kept his promise, although the feel of his hard body had been an unsettling experience. Yet she'd still fallen asleep…

The bunk dipped as his weight left it, leaving her curiously chilled. As if he read her mind, Vayne flipped the covering over her.

"Are you able to wait until I cleanse?"

"Yes." She really had to pee, but she was damned if she'd fall victim to any kind of syndrome, aware of how a twisted relationship could develop between kidnapper and the kidnapped, based on pathetic need and gratitude for the slightest kindness. She would never again fall into that trap.

"I require your *respect*, little…Neira."

Damn. He'd just undermined her, giving in to her request from the night before not to call her any pet names. And she hadn't missed the subtle, silky threat of correction when she'd sworn at him the previous evening, either. This man—this alien—wasn't to be trifled with or pushed too far. She had much to learn about him. Long gone were the days when she thought she could escape on her own or evade with merely her physical skills. Being a prisoner of war taught a harsh lesson, and one she'd take to her grave.

With an effort, not entirely feigned, considering the energy expended outside the lift on the *Astris* after months away from soldiering, Neira rolled over and looked him square in the eye. It was like taking a punch to the gut. The sovereign seemed even taller than the day before, and his muscled chest flowed easily into a flat, corded abdomen and long, equally muscled legs. Maybe his feet were toad ugly. She tried to skip over the evidence of his blatant masculinity but was unable to look away from his wide cock slapping unashamed at his belly, heavy sac drawn up beneath it. He'd shucked his garment before bed, or in the night. It struck her how...*human* he appeared, if larger than life. She supposed she wanted to see some definite differences, the better to set him apart from her.

Her own sex expressed its interest and appreciation, responding to this unapologetic male, dampening and plumping despite the direction from her brain to cease and desist. Had it been that long since she'd had a sexual relationship? It had. And for damn good reason. While she had the vagrant thought that something she had never thought to feel again had awoken in her, Neira worked hard at convincing herself any hot body would bring about the same response. And while she was at it, she tried to craft a verbal one with *respect* as its filler.

"I'm fine, thank you. I can wait. Sir." The sarcasm was faint and she wondered if he heard it.

With a grave nod, Vayne nodded and turned away, but not before she saw the flicker of amusement in his eyes. The bugger had set her up. Well, she was human. And he wasn't.

That sudden reminder took her breath. He was Shadalla. And royalty to boot. Sure, he looked like most human men, yet on that grander, larger scale, his cock included. But his features were ever-so-slightly suggestive of something else. Something different. Neira struggled to hold on to the impression, but it skittered away. The rumors and supposed facts flooded her forebrain but were too fragmented to sort through, especially under the impact of this virile male. All her briefings had been comprised of pertinent military information, without the gossipy snippets to flesh things out, and aside from the ribald sexual comments, mostly speculation. Almost as if her superiors hadn't wanted the troops to see the Shadalla as anything other than an arm's length ally. She hadn't been old enough to be in the actual war with the aliens before they signed the treaty and joined with Earth against the Juxtant, and she'd never fought alongside any.

The sovereign was indeed handsome, with rough-hewn cheekbones, a strong nose, and chiseled lips. His eyes were set widely, thickly lashed, and of a peculiar shade of blue. She was no girly girl and had limited experience with fashion and other such items outside of her military life, but Neira had seen the blue of the last pure sea on the Home World before the toxic blasts, and she thought Vayne's eyes could be compared to that. Turquoise, maybe, with flecks of— Shit! She was supposed to be trying to form an understanding of something that had teased at her well-honed senses, not go all loopy and start envisioning the alien as some kind of poster boy or something.

Her thoughts turned to the other women on board, and she wondered what their fate might be. Vayne hadn't touched her, personally, if one didn't count the press of his body against hers, probably all night long. Every time she woke, he was *there* and there'd been no space to retreat to, so she'd endured, at last sleeping deeply and well. But that didn't mean the rest of the female passengers weren't even now being ravished. Used. Despite his statement that there wouldn't be any *breeding*, at least not immediately. And just what the hell had that meant?

The bleak memory of her other prisoner-of-war situation flirted at the edge of her conscious mind but she refused to allow it access. The Home World, Earth to many, wasn't at war with anyone—at the moment—and was barely able to protect itself as it was, should there be another invasion. Not that they were advertising that fact. So she and the others wouldn't technically be considered prisoners, merely replaceable workers. And unless one or more of them had any ties to important persons back home, well, it was unlikely any rescue attempt would be mounted. If the businessmen who lost their cargo were inclined to seek out the perpetrators, Neira figured it would be the pirates they'd be searching for. Besides, the Shadalla were allies. There was a treaty. Right. They wouldn't even be considered prisoners of war to be ransomed.

With an irritable sigh, she eased into a more comfortable position and stared at the hull. This ship wasn't that different than the *Astris*, if a lot smaller, with curved outer walls and no portholes to be seen. Vayne's cabin was larger than her quarters on the disabled ship but as Spartan in its amenities. One would have thought royalty would've been entitled to something far more luxurious. The bed was comfortable, but it was hardly spacious. The new reminder of how she and her kidnapper had been pressed together so closely in the night made her cheeks heat, and she impatiently thrust that aside as well. He'd already told her what her future held, and she'd do well to be formulating a plan to foil him. She was no broodmare, although her fertility hadn't been compromised as far as she knew, despite what…*don't go there, Neira. Just don't.* She simply had no interest in a husband, let alone a kidnapping, alien husband. She had no emotional interest in sex, truth to be told, and no recent physical interest, even if Vayne was

ALLYSON YOUNG

sex on the proverbial stick.

"I will arrange for another meal."

Her heart thumped in her chest. She hadn't heard him approach, and that frightened her. What scared her more was the way her skin prickled at his proximity. She stared at him, determined not to show anything other than implacable calm. She donned her battle face, and thought she might have managed it, despite how his bare chest drew her eyes like a magnet. All that rippling muscle and golden skin… She swallowed, her mouth dry as dust, and fought against the weakness invading her. What on Earth? *That's the point, Neira. He is nothing on Earth and it stands to reason there is something else operating here to attract you.*

Now wearing what passed for underwear, Vayne somehow looked more naked than when he'd sauntered, totally nude, to the cleansing chamber. As in the night before, the garment sat low on his narrow hips, drawing attention to that ridge of muscle only very fit humanoid males developed. And in turn, that V shape drew the eye to what the fabric covered. Neira resolutely dragged her gaze up to his face—and the dagger he held pinched between two fingers of the hand resting up against the doorframe.

"If you care to use the facilities now, Neira…" She supposed there was no need for any more conversation. She was damned if she'd acknowledge the small weapon, annoyed with herself for not having hidden it better. She was also certain he would have accepted her attempt at such subterfuge. All prisoners reserved the right to try and escape. It was an unwritten rule across cultures—species—although the reaction to the attempts varied. The sovereign's body language didn't denote any violent intent, so she relaxed, a little surprised she could read him so well.

With a nod, she shifted to allow him access to the cuffs, watching him set the dagger down across the room.

"I'll store this with your interesting baton, little warrior. At some point they'll be returned to you, and perhaps you'll spar with me."

Biting her cheek to stave off an unconsidered response, like saying she'd take that opportunity to beat the ever-loving shit out of him, she concentrated on keeping space between them as he freed her. But she couldn't avoid the feather light trace of calloused fingertips down her forearms that made her want to shiver. And when he rubbed her wrists where the cuffs had caused some slight reddening, she had to bite harder to control a more visceral reaction.

She reminded her body again that any attractive male could take the edge off, if pure fucking was suddenly back on her menu, and that this one wanted far more than she was prepared to offer. Or was capable of, for that matter. Neira was desperately aware of her own fragile emotional state. She was totally unsuited to be anyone's lifemate, let alone a mother.

She tugged free and slid past him, unsure if he'd allow it, and wondering what she would do if he didn't. He was definitely having some kind of effect on her, and the loss of control made her want to scream. If she did that she wouldn't be able to stop. The breath she didn't know she'd been holding huffed out of her in an audible *whoosh*. She gained the cleansing room without any interference and huddled on the commode, shaking with repressed adrenaline and hoping Vayne wouldn't invade her privacy.

At length she regrouped and, after a wary look at the door, examined her face in the polished metal above the small sink. She could see it. The terrified, frantic animal behind the façade she'd painstakingly rebuilt after the team had stumbled upon her and Alexi Petrov. It had taken months of self-discipline and military-enforced therapeutic input to regain herself, or at least what passed for Neira Grekov. The therapy itself, with the intrusive machines and psychotropic medications, had been nearly as bad as what she'd experienced at the hands of the Juxtant. Maybe worse, because she well knew her former bosses weren't interested in her recovery so much as painting a soothing public relations picture. But they'd succeeded in repressing her memories, or at the very least giving her the tools to combat them—until now.

If those vids featuring her rescue and subsequent return to the Home World hadn't been splashed across the tabloids, she had no doubt she'd be in the same place as Petrov. Put down like an animal beyond hope and buried deep. Instead, she'd been the poster child for the military for a brief time, a hero, the prodigal daughter, all those terms to make the public feel warm and reassured. Alexi Petrov hadn't even been noticed as they featured her as the commander in the trenches of that final push against the Juxtant. One of theirs brought home from the enemy to the bosom of her soldier family, to be treated and cured. Healed. *Right.*

Securing her discharge had been a dance, orchestrated with the aid of a very skilled military lawyer and the threat of the truth coming out. The threat of certain hidden away materials to be released to the press should the military refuse to let her go. She would be eternally grateful to the friends she still retained among the ranks and the way they stood by her—and organized and documented the evidence for her to utilize if the need arose. She still felt guilty for using the evidence of Alexi's murder at the order of her superiors to secure her own escape, but the alternative forced her hand. There was no way she could have stayed in that life and be reminded each and every day of her failure.

Her disappearance from the *Astris* would create considerable relief across the board, and this time her superiors would keep a lid on the news. No one would even know she was gone. The frightened part of her blinked out, cast back into the shadows. Following that relief, utter sadness overwhelmed her.

"Neira?"

His voice interrupted the painful trip down memory lane and headed off a very probable topple into the abyss. Being taken and held against her will was indeed unlocking all the carefully locked and guarded doors and dismantling her shields. Kidnapped…and something else she couldn't seem to defend against, at least not until she successfully identified it. But it definitely was emanating from this Shadalla and she *was* losing control. What if that frightened part escaped its binds?

"I'll be right out."

The face regarding her above the sink cracked in a twisted smile. So domestic. So accommodating. *I'll be right out. Darling. Sweetheart.* Like she had any choice. The feeling of being powerless gnawed at her and on impulse she hammered both hands against her thighs, the dull pain serving to ground her as she curled her toes against the floor. She sucked in two huge draughts of air and straightened her spine. She was made of sterner stuff than this.

Vayne regarded her from an indolent pose near the bunk as she entered his quarters. She could see the sexual interest written large across his handsome face, and once again that feminine part of her tried to escape her sensible side. At least he was dressed—in the same style of uniform he affected the previous day, though his boots were different. The new footwear was more suited for space travel than for boarding vessels that might have lost their gravitational integrity, she supposed.

Her nudity had never bothered her before. She'd been naked around both men and women in barracks and in the showers for much of her career. And she'd been kept mostly naked as a captive, basic confinement 101, something she'd been trained to endure, along with other things. Things she didn't care to think about. Things that had actually happened, in addition to other forms of torture no one had considered. But she was absurdly aware of how *unclothed* she felt in front of this male. Not vulnerable, exactly, certainly not humiliated, so she supposed *unsettled* was the best way to describe it. He made her feel very aware of herself as a woman, and that wouldn't do.

With her head high, she met his stare and watched those turquoise-blue eyes shimmer with refracted light before they darkened in a manner that made her twitch. He nodded at the bunk and she forced herself to look in that direction. The coverings were pulled up and tucked in tightly, and she thought perhaps a servant had attended him while she was having her mini breakdown in the latrine. Because surely a sovereign didn't stoop to such mundane tasks.

"Please sit," he invited, and she skirted him, hopefully without being too obvious about it, to perch on the edge of the mattress. His scent and heat enveloped her as he leaned to tether her wrists yet again. It was getting old, but she was damned if she'd let him think it bothered her. Better he come to allow her freedom on his own when she could use the element of surprise. Surely at some point he would relax his guard.

Vayne kept his gaze on her face, but she was only too aware of the way his underclothing tented over an enormous erection.

To distract herself, she said, "I'm hungry."

"You didn't eat much yesterday," he agreed. He reached to a tray on the small table. It spoke to how distracting he was that she hadn't even noticed the food. He offered up a folded piece of a bread-like substance. Bright red fruit coated the end, and her taste buds salivated in anticipation.

With her hands secured, it was awkward to reach for the sustenance, and to her surprise he placed the offering against her lips. Feeling remarkably like a child being fed by a doting parent, she nipped at the food and nearly closed her eyes in joy when the taste of something quite like fresh strawberries burst over her tongue.

The sovereign smiled and tucked another piece between her parted lips. "It's my favorite too, Neira. We are able to grow the fruit in abundance in certain areas on Nibiru."

She swallowed and managed not to smile back, wishing she could feed herself. Undeterred, he continued to provide her with mouthfuls of the bread and preserve, balanced with sips of a hot beverage that tasted a lot like strong, sweet tea. He didn't touch his own dish until he was assured she was full, and she strove to keep her guard up. Her kidnapper wasn't going to soften her resolve by caring for her.

"I would like to spend the day getting to know you."

She could refuse, she supposed. Refuse to cooperate in any way, but then she might lose an opportunity to learn something that could conceivably lead to escape at some point, if not deter him from his goal. She nodded, working hard at not seeing how the pleased grin he gave her added immeasurably to his attractiveness. Were her brains turning to mush?

And so began the dance. It reminded Neira of a

preliminary interrogation, one she turned out to be on the wrong side of—again. But she parried and deflected all his questions, from one as simple as a request for her last name, to one inquiring about her family. The latter pricked a little bubble of pain and regret. Being an orphan and having lost track of her two younger sisters during the war wasn't something she wanted to think, or talk, about. It was interesting that she couldn't drum up a sense of outrage against Vayne and the role his kind had played in that war. She hated her superiors far more, especially when it had come to light how the powers that be had refused the hand the Shadalla offered in friendship and initially attacked, instead. Xenophobic bastards, all of them.

"What can it hurt to tell me your last name, Neira? And share about your family?"

"I've told you, Sovereign. I'm your prisoner and the less you know about me, the better. I have no interest in sharing anything as personal as my family with you."

His affable mask slipped, and she tensed inwardly, waiting for the punishment she anticipated, but she saw only mild frustration. "Then perhaps you have questions of me."

"Why can't I have my clothes?"

The way his stare slipped over her body caused a quiver, and her core heated enough to make her thighs flex in an effort to contain her arousal. There was nothing she could do about her beading nipples.

"Because I like looking at what is mine. And you can't hide from me. Your body tells me much of what I need to know."

****

Vayne hadn't missed the effect he was having on his little warrior, despite how determined she appeared to reject him. Her feminine self was well on the way to recognizing its counterpart in his maleness, and while he could admit to frustration at her strong emotional resistance, would he want a mate to be any different? The three other men on board fortunate enough to find a chosen were reporting similar opposition, if not with such stubbornness. He did his best to ignore a flicker of conscience, for while the chase was stimulating, this Neira wouldn't be the one who'd be his eventual lifemate. A subdued, compliant version of her would surely be just as appealing. Surely it would…

He watched her bring herself under control and could only guess at the effort, so skilled was she at hiding. So much to learn.

"I'm not yours, Sovereign. You're deluding yourself."

"I've ruled for several decades now, Neira. My people are long lived, if prone to losses in succession. I've fought in two wars and have seen things in this quadrant that shook my faith and challenged my sanity, but when it comes to you, I'm not delusional. Shadalla know when they find their chosen."

"How does your kind know?" Her lips were set in definite askance.

He didn't like the way she tried to distance them—his kind versus hers. There was little difference between their actual DNA, and he supposed the genetic seeds planted on Nibiru and those on her Home World were from the same source, as was the case in much of this system. With some mutations. And hadn't that extra heart come in handy for him?

"Our bodies have a response." At her repressed snort, he shook his head. "Not just my cock's reaction to your lovely body, Neira. Any healthy male would respond to that. I'm talking about something in the brain that awakens and telegraphs a message to its host."

"What kind of message?"

"I could possibly describe it as a feeling of total and utter need to possess, to protect, to…cherish."

He hadn't intended to be quite so impassioned and descriptive but thought it might be worth it, considering the way Neira's eyes widened and a faint flush stole up over her throat to paint her cheeks. For an instant he thought he witnessed a hint of moisture behind her suddenly lowered lashes.

If he had, it wasn't apparent when she fluttered them open and fixed him with a stare. "And if your *chosen* doesn't feel the same?"

"It doesn't work that way, Neira. There are no mistakes."

"Maybe not with your kind. But I'm not Shadalla."

Never one to admit defeat, he still had the urge to upend her and smack her curvaceous bottom—just to see the bloom of color on her skin and hear her breathy moans. Stubborn female. "We have the same effect on Earth females, Neira. The results are very positive, I assure you."

"So the rumors are true, then. There are other Earth—Home World—women on Nibiru."

This conversation wasn't going the way he'd planned, but he would never outright lie to his chosen. Omission wasn't exactly lying. "There are. They…arrived before the treaty, and afterward, once we discovered the genetic weapon. And before you question me, they are all placed with their lifemates, and none have regretted it. Not one have asked to leave and return to the Home World."

Neira shrugged, making her breasts jiggle enticingly. His mouth nearly watered with his need to suckle the tight red nipples. "I guess I find that hard to believe. People on Earth regret their relationships all the time."

Pitching his voice lower and locking his gaze on hers, he replied, "As you have taken great pains to point out, the Shadalla are different from your kind. We mate for life, unless one fades, and there is no reason to think our connection with Earth females will be any different."

As he'd hoped, her mouth softened, and she leaned toward him. "When you say fades…does that mean *dies*?"

She leaned away on the last word and he sighed inwardly. Patience was not one of his virtues where Neira was concerned. "It does. We believe our souls fade into the cosmos."

"I'm not sure I have a soul."

As a conversation stopper and a major distraction, Vayne couldn't think of anything that would have been more effective. And she clearly wished she hadn't shared it. Her lovely face assumed the remote expression he was tiring of. It resonated with despair deep within him he didn't wish to revisit, yet he longed to take it from her, absorb the hopelessness and spare her. She swiveled to draw her legs up and tucked them beneath her, curling sideways on the bunk. Gooseflesh peppered her skin and he snatched up an extra blanket, drifting it over her. He climbed onto the mattress, knowing enough to take a position behind her, despite his urge to take advantage of her vulnerability and make her face him.

He pressed against her, feeling how cool she'd become, and let his own heat seep into her until she relaxed a little and her breathing leveled out.

"Are you all right?"

Her reply was muffled but seemingly devoid of emotion. "I'm fine."

That four letter word clearly meant the same thing

from all females across the universe, and Vayne would be a fool to ignore its portent. And he was definitely not a fool. He chose to try and distract her. "Would you care to attend the exercise room?"

"Can I wear clothes?" Her voice was even now, and much clearer.

He swallowed down a growl, surprised at himself despite how strongly she affected him. "No one sees what is mine."

"Lord." But it was a faint protest, and he smiled.

Chapter Four

Neira stayed in the cleansing room as long as she dared. She'd just showered again, and not only to wash the sweat from her body but to deal with the slickness between her legs. The sense of losing control made her reluctant to see him again.

Vayne had been consistently invading her space, affording her no privacy except for her bodily functions. The stint in the exercise room, an interesting area filled with many of the accouterments she used in her own training, had settled her nerves with the familiar. Until she'd sparred with the sovereign. He was a warrior, as she'd assumed, and well trained. Even her quickness hadn't saved her, and the experience of his hands all over her, as well as the time she'd spent on the floor beneath his strong body, elicited those damn responses she couldn't keep tamped down. As for her fantasy about bringing him to his knees with her fighting ability...well, he hadn't allowed her the *palka*.

They'd even shared a meal in that training room, sitting on benches in a corner, Vayne choosing the best cuts of meat and vegetables to offer her. She had been hard pressed to ignore the speculative and appreciative glances of a few crew members who worked out in close proximity while keeping a respectful distance. The business of being fed from his hand meant things she didn't care to consider. The sovereign never took his focus from her and if she forgot herself and her situation for an instant, it was like basking in definite warmth.

She'd tried to stay alert for any opportunity to take advantage of but was fast becoming resigned to the fact she was on a ship in space, surrounded by Shadalla, and definitely with nowhere to run. So that meant she had to dissuade the alien and convince him she wasn't destined to be any part of his future.

Vayne took her on a tour of the *Tomodr*, and she'd soaked in the surroundings eagerly, though thwarted by the unfamiliar written language and markings. Not to mention being distracted by the big hand resting familiarly and possessively on the small of her back. He guided her with his touch, but it was more than that, and willing her body's responses away was become more and more difficult. She was beginning to doubt her ability to resist him, and the fear that invoked helped her find additional strength.

"Neira."

She quit stalling and sallied forth, glumly aware he'd filched her clothing again. A garment reposed on the bed. It appeared to be a dress of some sort, a long, flowing item of clothing in varying shades of white and cream. Something she would never choose for herself and something she was certain she didn't care to wear. Vayne was once again dressed in his uniform of leggings and tunic, his loose exercise clothing nowhere to be seen. She tore her gaze away from the sight of his tall, strong body.

"We will take the evening meal with the crew and their females, Neira, if you will don the *paca*. Three of your fellow passengers are chosens."

That sounded like too much of coincidence to her, and her resolve suddenly firmed. There was more to this chosen business than he was letting on. She'd actually begun to consider that it might be akin to miraculously finding one's soul mate amongst many, but perhaps it was like having a certain blood type.

"I'd prefer my own clothing." She didn't miss the slight flicker of irritation that tightened the skin around his mouth—and it served to have her take notice of how sculpted his lips were. *Focus!*

"My bride must be properly attired, Neira."

"I am not your bride."

His demeanor didn't change. "For all intents and purposes, you are. You will be. And I want you to meet more of my crew, dressed appropriately."

She could refuse, make a scene, but then what? She might be confined to the cabin and risk his ire, though she truly didn't sense he would harm her. And if she complied, she would be able to see the other captives and get some answers to her questions. Without acknowledging his imposing presence, she crossed to where the confounded dress lay. There were two scraps of fabric tucked alongside the skirt—underwear, and she spied footwear set primly on the floor, a weaving of straps over a thin sole in yet another shade of cream. Definitely a theme here, and one she really didn't want to think about. If he was in any way suggesting purity, he had another think coming.

****

Watching his little warrior slip into the undergarments he had pulled from where they were stored amongst his personal belongings made him impossibly hard despite the fact she donned them without fanfare or further protest. There was no artifice in Neira, no apparent need to tease or titillate, yet she was overwhelmingly sexy. He hadn't acknowledged the underlying hope that he might spy a chosen on this journey but somehow the *paca* had found its way to the trunk. It was designed to cover most any feminine person, and its enveloping folds would both shield and establish the sovereign's choice. What he wasn't prepared for was the way his hearts—even his damaged one—swelled in concert, or how his throat tightened at the sight of the symbolic garment dropping past Neira's proud head to flow over and shroud her tall, slender form. She was born to this.

He took the two steps necessary to reach her, putting out a hand to smooth the fabric over her shoulders, any pretext to touch her again and experience that indescribable feeling of possession. He forgot that her reaction to his impulsive move had been ingrained through intensive training, and because she was female, it mitigated his counter response. He very nearly lost the battle this time around. Neira feinted away from his outstretched fingers, then transferred her weight back toward him, a move barely telegraphed because of the enveloping folds of the garment. Vayne had only a fraction of a second to register that irony when a solid blow to his solar plexus took his breath and she drove upward to plant her skull against his jaw.

The blinding pain almost stole his control, and his animal persona surged to wick through the pores of his skin. Fighting a battle on two fronts, he struggled to take charge of his beast and stay present while subduing Neira. He felt her shudder as he wrapped her up and bore her to the floor under his superior weight. To his surprise, unlike her efforts in their sparring, she immediately surrendered, lying acquiescent beneath him while the very air in the room crackled and shimmered like a live being.

He carefully released her and straightened to his full height, watching her warily as he composed his features. She raised her head and struggled amongst the wealth of fabric to a sitting position before looking his way. Her stare was unapologetic, yet he detected a hint of something else buried deep in those remarkable eyes.

"You have no cause to fear me, Neira." He kept his voice calm and reassuring, uncertain of how much she'd seen or felt within him.

After an appreciable pause, she responded. "I'm a

little on edge. Being kidnapped and all. It's second nature to me to protect myself against unwanted touch."

Deciding to ignore the latter part of her comment, he gestured to the door. "Will you control yourself and accompany me?"

The flash of despair he witnessed made him wish to take it back, or at the very least pull her to him and soothe her angst. It felt all the more important to do so, seeing as he was responsible for it, but he knew to refrain.

On a deep breath, she answered, "I'm well aware there is nowhere to go, Sovereign. And I would see the other ca…women. I'll control myself."

"Only those women who have been chosen will be there, Neira. The others must wait until we arrive on Nibiru."

Stiffening, she glared at him. "Explain. I mean, why is that?"

He wondered what rank she had held, this fierce woman who had little patience for diplomacy. Had she given orders, expecting them to be followed without question? Had she followed those from her superiors? But she was trying not to alienate him, that was clear, and he reflected he had yet to earn her respect. Although he should demand it, considering his status and the one he had conferred, simply by choosing her. He set that aside.

"Some of the crew volunteered for this mission in the hope of finding a lifemate, Neira. But of course not all of them spied one. There were only thirteen Earth females…found, remember." He thought that sounded better than captured or kidnapped, but from the look on her face she thought differently.

"So you're sequestering the rest?"

"As is our custom."

A faint snort escaped her, quite out of keeping

with her formerly stoic mannerisms. "Your custom. Not ours. Not theirs. It makes me wonder what in hell they're thinking about. And how frightened they must be. And what of the women who were *chosen*? Do *they* have a choice? Or are they like me?"

Maintaining his control, Vayne ticked off his answers. "Regarding the first of your concerns, I can only assure you those females being sequestered are being provided with everything they need and also given all appropriate information. Their questions are being answered and they have time to prepare for what awaits on Nibiru. I've heard of no worrisome responses. And the chosen... Consider them as arranged marriages favored on your planet eons ago, Neira." At her faint look of surprise, he shrugged. "I am interested in the history of many worlds. In any event, I assure you none of them, or you, will come to any harm—"

"Except we've all had our power taken away, lost our families and contact with everything familiar. To *breed* more Shadalla. To *pay* for the perfidy of those who rule the Home World."

Her anger and bitterness cut him. Stiffly, he responded, "You will all be cared for beyond anything you thought or believed possible."

"Uh-huh." Her disdain grated, and he mostly kept his temper if only with great effort, but still he lashed out.

"You will have nothing but time to learn I speak the truth." The cold, inflexible fact obviously struck her as hard as any blow might have done. He witnessed the shock and another flicker of despair as she turned away and sat heavily on the bed.

Regret now colored his perception, but there was nothing more he could do but show her the new way of life she might expect. "Accompany me, Neira."

"I'm not hungry."

"I won't allow you to sulk in my quarters like a child." He daren't leave her alone, not knowing the lengths she would go to in her efforts to avoid the inevitable. His comment had the desired effect. He was already learning much about his intended, aware she would respond to his inference from the depths of her proud, lovely form. She stood, preceding him to the door. The *paca* didn't conceal her angry movements.

****

Vayne couldn't remember a more unpleasant meal. The rations were that of a warship, of course, and not particularly fine fare, but it wasn't the food. Neira projected an icy aura he felt powerless to breach, surrounded by members of his crew and three of the other women from the *Astris*, along with their males. He couldn't fault the way she presented herself, unfailingly polite to those off-duty members, solicitous with the women who looked intently to her for direction.

Leric's fair-haired female had been quivering in her seat at his exec's right hand, wearing the pale blue colors of his particular calling. She'd taken her cue from Neira and had calmed but turned from any attention offered by Leric. The same thing applied to the two slight, brown-haired women wearing coral and gold, respectively, chosen for the navigator and one of the weapons' officers. Vayne preferred to see their fear and anxiety drain away, of course, and leave room for their higher functions to begin to assess and understand their situation, but there was no balance in this. They should be drawing strength from their mates, embracing the bonding process, as Neira should be looking to him. He ruefully accepted he needed to rethink things, look past the bone-deep attraction and be more instructional with his chosen bride. It renewed his determination not to speak fully of the holding period, and he was relieved to remember his crew had already been advised to keep certain aspects of that custom private.

"How long do we have to stay on Nibiru?" Leric's blonde bride, Victoria, directed the question to Neira, yet surely his exec had been honest with his chosen.

"I've been informed that planet will be our home from here on in, Vicky." Neira spoke calmly and gently, as behooved a sovereign's mate, but he heard something throb deep in her tone.

"But I don't want—"

"I have explained this to you, my bride," Leric interjected, gently placing his hand on Victoria's forearm. Vayne was gratified to see the young female initially relax at his executive officer's touch, but she then pulled away and stared harder at Neira.

"I want to return home."

"Me too."

"Same."

The agreement came in a soft chorus from Sheera and Alondra, and he watched their men's lips tighten. Eltrast sent him a glance and flicked a similar one toward Neira. Clearly the weapons' officer had expected Vayne to have already convinced his own chosen to accept her fate and encourage the other brides to follow suit, to lead by example. Vayne swallowed down a strange urge to laugh—it appeared the sovereign wasn't all powerful and knowing when it came to his female.

"We aren't allowed to spend time together," Neira said softly. "I suspect our hosts fear we'll plot against them."

Vayne was on his feet, reaching to tug her up and escort her back to their quarters, when she continued. "But I was a soldier, and I don't pretend to understand such relationships. Romantic ones. However, the Home World won't be sending anyone to rescue us, because they won't know where to begin to look. The Shadalla are our allies, remember, so Nibiru will be the last place they'll consider." The faint irony in her tone was overshadowed by how earnest she sounded.

"The sovereign has promised that none of you will be harmed, and in fact will be treated extremely well. I don't mean to undermine your hope, but sometimes it's important to accept what you can't change and embrace it if you can," she carried on, and Vayne found himself sitting again with no memory of doing so.

"Leric told me most of that," Victoria said. "But I didn't know what to believe. I wanted to believe him…"

The other two women nodded and cast glances at their mates, though Vayne thought he detected a certain warmth in their looks.

Jurlek's female added, "I wondered if they took us to pay back the military and the politicians for what they did. The genetic disease, I mean, that Jurlek told me about. But then I realized we don't mean anything to the people back home. We were all sent out on the *Astris* because we have nobody. Nothing to return to, no reason to return."

Vayne registered the faint tremor in his chosen mate and noted her sudden pallor. He stood again and nodded to those around the tables. "It is as my bride has shared. You will be revered as lifemates, our brides, and very well treated. You will want for nothing."

Neira didn't protest as he clasped her elbow and urged her to her feet. She hadn't touched any of the food before her. The faint smile she gave the other women didn't encompass his crew—those she gave a quick inclination of her head. He had the sensation his little warrior was holding on to her control by the tiniest measure.

Vayne spoke over his shoulder, directly to the

females. "We may speak more at tomorrow's evening meal, and I would hope you discuss any further concerns with your mates and formulate additional questions."

Walking Neira back to their quarters was like escorting a mechanical being. Her slender form was rigid and moved with nothing of her usual grace. And it wasn't his imagination that she felt cold—colder than that morning. Her body was like a barometer, reflecting her state of mind. He kept silent as they passed various crew members going about their duties, noting their curious—and envious—glances, behind the obeisance.

He released her upon entering the sleeping room, and she halted immediately, staring straight ahead. A deeper flicker of worry lashed his senses and he was uncertain if he should touch her.

"Please remove the *paca*, Neira."

With jerky movements, she complied. Keeping a wary eye on her, he rummaged through his stores until he found another long garment for her to don. He'd often keep her naked when they were in his home, but he sensed she required clothing at this moment.

Taking the *paca* from her hands in order to put it safely away, he passed her the dark length of material and was relieved to see her tug it over her head without comment or visible reaction. His relief was immediately replaced with anxiety and he decided to address it.

"Tell me what is wrong, Neira."

Again, there was nothing coy about her, no prevarication. Yet she wouldn't meet his eyes. "I just told three women to lay down their arms and surrender, accept the inevitable."

"And that was the best thing, the correct thing to do." He wouldn't admit he might see it differently, had it been him taken and en route to an alien planet to mate with strangers and continue their line. He did what he had to do.

"I don't have to like it." Her voice quavered slightly.

"Ah, my bride…I am sorry. But I must do what is right for my people."

"And what does that make me? And the other twelve women on this ship?" She nearly whispered her questions.

Vayne stared at her, uncertain. This female again unsettled him. "I don't understand—"

"*Your people*, Sovereign. What are *we* to you?"

"You will be my people too, Neira," he said as gently as he could and leaned to put his arms around her, seeking to offer comfort.

"Don't. Touch. Me." The words were delivered with venom anointing every syllable.

"You are my bride. And to be the mother of my children. Of course I will have to touch you." After her reassuring, albeit brief, speech to the other women, he was at a loss as to her response. He'd assumed, despite the way she'd retreated, that she'd included herself in that helpful speech.

She finally lifted those golden eyes to stare into his. "Then you'll do it against my will, without my consent. And your children won't have a mother. In truth, I'll be merely a vessel."

His other self came surging from the depths and writhed against the barrier of his skin. It had happened twice now in this woman's company, and that part of him never surfaced unless on the battlefield. Shock and dismay warred with outrage and fury, and he clung to his control. He thought they had come farther… "As you say, little warrior. But I assure you, you'll be longing for my touch and begging for my seed. And children will be borne of our joining, strong and willful warriors. Your maternal skills won't be required."

Her gaze searched his and once again he saw her go, retreat someplace deep inside her he thought he might never find. Dark, pained resignation. The blazing amber of her irises faded and leached into a pale facsimile, and for the first time in a very, very long time, Lord Vayne Palldyn, Sovereign of the Southern Range, planet Nibiru, Shadalla, wondered if he'd finally reached the end of his vast capabilities. Foiled by a female, one half his size and not even of Nibiru.

Chapter Five

Vayne left his quarters, and Neira supposed it was because she'd drawn the line in the sand with her earlier impassioned assertion about him having to take from her what he wanted, by force. She'd meant it and she'd stand by it. But at the same time it made her feel like a total hypocrite, reassuring Vicky, Sheera and Alondra, *encouraging* them to accept the kidnapping and subsequent life with the alien men who had chosen them. Implying that producing children to repopulate Nibiru wasn't such a bad deal, when she personally had no intention of complying.

She told herself it was necessary to do what she'd done. It was like being in charge of a division of new recruits, looking out for their best interests and giving them good direction. But a leader didn't ask troops to do anything they themselves wouldn't do, and in this case she simply couldn't. She could barely manage to keep her roiling emotions in check as they fought to be released, constantly triggered as they were in this situation. Because it wasn't like she would react in any predictable way, arousal be damned. Where were those medications she'd eschewed upon leaving the military, now when she needed them most?

Intellectually, she knew that the Shadalla weren't like the Juxtant. At least she thought they weren't. They were much the same size and coloring, but the Juxtant were fearsome and loathsome to look upon, their features vulpine, black eyes dark and soulless, and their barbarism knew no bounds. And the Shadalla allied with the Home World to defeat their common enemy, so she could believe there was a considerable difference. Except Vayne had broken the treaty. *With good reason,* a tiny voice in her head argued. *Genocide is heinous.* Ignoring the inner commentary, she considered the fact of the restraints on his bunk. The Juxtant favored bindings as well…and other things. She pushed past that and wondered if the sovereign anticipated the need to bind his lifemate, that she wouldn't be willing. It might explain the eyebolts. Or it might not.

They were well placed, in any event. She was once again in the cuffs and tethered to the bunk, gathered up in an eye blink after her ultimatum and efficiently secured. Vayne had moved with such speed and determination she'd only managed a token resistance. At least she was clothed, if in another one of those loose, shapeless dresses that covered her from beneath her chin to the floor, over the comfortable underwear.

He'd left her there without additional commentary, and she had settled after a while to consider her predicament. For certain she'd made things more difficult for herself but took consolation in believing the other women she spoke to were in better emotional shape as a result. Her thoughts turned to the rest, sequestered someplace on the ship. They had to be frightened no matter how Palldyn reassured her. Would it help them to hear what she'd said to the other three? Alondra's words came back to her and she wondered if it was significant that all the passengers on the *Astris* had no one back home. It had been the other woman's comments that struck home to point out just how truly alone Neira was, and it all became too much.

Her mind worried over the thought until the door panel hissed open and Vayne strode inside. Despite her banked anger, her traitorous body once again woke up and took notice. Had *he* noticed how difficult it had been for her to reject his touch? It was like her bones melted and her muscles went lax when he came close, desire pooling between her legs as her breasts ached and her nipples pinched into painful nubs. Even the simplest drift or clasp of his fingers shut all her good sense down—until the lack of control unlocked her terror. Everything was then washed aside in the deluge, and she couldn't consider what being bound to this alien would mean: the loss of her whole self. *Never.* She hadn't given over to the Juxtant, and Vayne wasn't going to break her, either, despite the difference in his technique and what he wanted from her. Because, in the end, it meant the same thing. Total surrender. Trapped in that cycle forever.

Her traitorous body worked harder to prepare her for him as he approached, even though her arousal cooled a tad when he wordlessly stripped her of the shapeless clothing as well as the undergarments, ignoring her efforts to retain them. He ripped the fabric free rather than loosen the cuffs, and his mastery both titillated and terrified her. Madness. After tucking her beneath the cover of the bunk, he climbed in to take up his usual position behind her.

"Sleep well, little warrior. We have much to discuss tomorrow."

Like she could drop off after that comment. Squirming into a more comfortable position, she tormented herself by counting his heartbeats, a strange echo causing her to lose track. She thought she sensed when he fell asleep, his deeper breaths ruffling her hair—a curiously intimate sensation. For a moment she allowed herself to entertain the idea of belonging to a man like Vayne, to have a purpose in life again, if a very different one, and the shard of pain penetrating her chest literally took her breath. Perhaps flirting with insanity wasn't such a good idea. She slipped into an uneasy slumber on that thought.

****

Vayne woke her with a press on her shoulder and she struggled into awareness to see him standing beside the bunk, fully dressed. It wasn't like her to be unaware of movement around her while she slept and she hadn't even awakened when he'd left their bed. His bed. Her throat felt tight and she tried to swallow against the sensation. She was losing her edge. Without a word, he released her cuffs and stepped back, his big body clearly alert for any acting out. She worked her arms to alleviate the stiffness, stupidly wishing for his earlier actions to soothe them, before slipping from the bunk to hurry to the cleansing room. Vayne's flat affect and expressionless face made her more uncomfortable than she cared to admit, and when she emerged to see him regarding her just as impassively, she had to fight down an insane urge to apologize.

"Please sit." His courtesy was at odds with his cool demeanor.

Blinking, she saw the food arranged on a tray beside the bed and made to go to the chair alongside. He shook his head and gestured to the bunk. Confused, she sat where he indicated, and he pulled the chair forward, dropping into it.

"Must I cuff you?" It sounded so offhand, careless.

"No. I'll behave." And there was that need to please again, like a child acknowledging the loving supremacy of the other being in the room. Dependent on him for everything.

She watched as he carefully loaded an eating utensil with some morsels of meat and a vegetable and raised it to her lips. He was back to feeding her, and there was no reason for it.

Leaning back, she said, "I can feed myself."

Vayne shrugged, and the food fell from the fork to

the plate. "It is our tradition for the holding period."

"What's that, this holding period?" At least he was talking to her, although why that should matter was beyond her. She certainly wasn't rethinking her edict.

There was no guile in those turquoise-blue eyes as he answered, but she still had a sense he was withholding. Maybe lying by omission. "It's a period of time in which Shadalla males court our chosen, accustom them to our individual personalities—learn about the other."

"Like dating?" Not that she had ever dated. She hadn't had the time or the opportunity. Sexual contact had been spontaneous and her partners usually from the ranks. It hadn't seemed to matter if she saw them outside of soldiering. What she knew of them was important enough—she knew them as warriors, men to have your back, trustworthy and stalwart. They always used protection—easily available to the troops—and any intimacy came from the bond forged through combat and nothing else. There had been nothing to compare to the incredible appeal this Shadalla held for her.

"Similar to your dating process, I suppose. We are somewhat more…intense." He offered her another forkful of food and fixed her with a calm stare.

Extremely hungry, the evening meal ignored despite his efforts to provide for her, she slowly parted her lips. Her hands lifted at the same time but subsided to the coverlet at the nearly indiscernible shake of his head. Well, she'd promised.

The flavors of the food burst over her tongue and she swept it off the fork to chew and swallow rapidly. It was foreign, being fed by his hand once again, but at least they weren't at one another's throats. The fear she harbored and kept under desperate control then stretched a little and began to raise its head. *You are giving up your power, soldier.* She breathed deeply, and the scent of

Vayne, something clean and earthy, doused her terror and silenced the eerie voice. She was able to accept another mouthful, and another, until she was full, sipping at the cup of ale he offered afterward.

The enigmatic look on his face gave her pause, but she thanked him politely and was rewarded with a slight curl of those appealing lips. She found herself leaning forward, involuntarily, and jerked back, and whatever had been building between them was broken. He sighed.

"You'll be restrained at night, and while I am on duty—"

"I understand you think I'll try to do you harm in your sleep," she said, unable to hide her scorn. "But what kind of trouble do you think I can get into alone in here? There's no access to anything important." She'd scanned the area closely, so she knew. The screen on the wall wasn't accessible to anything other than his thumbprint, so she wouldn't be able to even gather information. "And if you fear I'll lie in wait for you...I'm well aware of the Shadalla's policy about hostages." They never negotiated. Ever. There might be an exception made in the case of the sovereign, however.

"I'm not concerned about you causing trouble or lying in wait, little warrior."

She chafed at the nickname but supposed he was within his rights after the barrier she'd thrown up between them earlier. He hadn't called her Neira since. "So what's the issue?"

"I won't allow you to harm yourself as you consider your limited options."

The figurative hand squeezing her belly made her regret the meal she'd consumed, and she couldn't seem to catch her breath. She contented herself with a raised eyebrow and hoped she didn't look as stunned as she felt.

When? How had he seen her ever-present, weary hope for death?

"Do you think I haven't paid attention to my chosen? That I haven't seen and felt the despair you strive to hide? Will you tell me your story so I might completely take your pain?"

Her belly released in an anguished gush of sensation and she broke out in a fine sweat, unable to break away from his intent stare. Her hands scrabbled at the coverlet and found enough purchase to lever her weight and allow her to back away slightly. The heat of his gaze stretched out between them, as strong a tether as the one attached to his bed, and she couldn't break free from it either.

She hung there, poised between telling him, sharing her deepest, most shameful secrets, or subsiding into the depths and hugging the agony to herself, when the com on the display sounded. The male voice spoke in a dialect her translator failed to interpret, but Vayne's body stiffened and he muttered in the same language. She fell backward on the bed. Her quivering, shaking form seemed to belong to someone else as she pretended relief he'd backed off. Regardless, concern etched his features.

"Breathe, little warrior." His big palms swept over her arms and down her sides and eased the shivers, and she became aware he was tucking the cover around her, sealing in some warmth. He attached the cuffs and whispered an apology, but she detected his resolve as she gained a modicum of control. Had he given her that merely by his touch?

"I have something to attend to I am unable to ignore, but I will be back to discuss the other reasons for your restraints. The more…pleasurable ones."

She peered after him as he strode from the room, not at all distracted by the other reasons he referenced.

He'd done it to address her upset reaction, and indeed she had established a little more control. She already knew what he alluded to and hadn't pulled any punches when she called him a pervert. Though he'd have to go a long way to top the Juxtant… She yanked her thoughts away from that direction and focused on the fact he'd gotten into her head after only two days. There *had* to be something else operating here. Hadn't she thought that earlier? She cast her mind back to all those briefings she'd attended and flipped through any and all extraneous information she'd stored in her brain in regard to the Shadalla. But try as she might, she couldn't come up with anything regarding mind control or Shadalla mating rituals.

****

Vayne cursed again, this time far louder, as he loped toward the bridge access. Leric would have spoken the old language—one not easily translated by the universal translator—for good reason, and he hadn't used Neira's name. Called her the sovereign's chosen. But the obvious importance of the summons resonated in Leric's voice. His exec was facing aft when Vayne burst onto the bridge, and whirled around, nodding in acknowledgment and respect.

"Sovereign, we've been monitoring as usual, and we didn't expect anything but picked up a long-range message from Captain Ristos. It's not completely clear, but he sends a warning. The Outriders of the *Astris* made extraordinary efforts to run him down, and he was nearly apprehended. It apparently took him some time to locate and secure the emergency pod he pursued, and it gave them the opportunity to get closer than one might expect."

"And what does this have to do with my chosen?" Vayne heard the deadly rage threading through his quiet question as his instincts kicked in, and so did Leric by the way his eyebrows shot up.

"The passenger on the pod provided some information about her, Sovereign, including her last name and some rumors, perhaps some facts. She was military as you believed, and discharged, but her superiors appear reluctant to lose sight of her. At least that is the reasoning suggested by the pirate captain. The cargo he, ah, liberated, negates such efforts of determined pursuit. It is easily replaced."

"Our Captain Ristos is an intelligent man," Vayne mused. "I tend to follow his reasoning. Unless one of the other females is connected in some way that the Home World would be so tenacious?"

Leric shrugged. "Ristos scanned the passenger manifest along with the cargo and was able to break the encryption. I accept responsibility for failing to even think of it."

"You had good reason, Leric. Your apology is noted." Vayne wouldn't hold the male's distraction against him, considering his own.

His exec inclined his head before continuing. "Your chosen was traveling under a different name, so perhaps that is why she is the only one with scanty information on her file, and you are aware how the Home World gathers every attainable piece of data on its inhabitants. I have begun the process of working through the data we…obtained…during out stint there."

Vayne ignored Leric's reference to the espionage the Shadalla had carried out on the poorly protected informational centers of the Home World during the treaty negotiations. The information had served them well, and continued to stream to Nibiru. It would take time to access it on the *Tomodr*. "And does Ristos believe the Outriders will widen the search or have an inkling of our involvement in the hijacking?"

The *Tomodr* was a fine warship, but they were still a considerable distance from Nibiru. And there was a large number of Outriders, ideal for both defense and offense. He mentally chastised himself for taking the slower route home but had hoped for additional time with Neira, for the holding period to take place within the confines of the ship. Where she would have fewer distractions and more reason to allow his attentions.

"He didn't say. The message is over a day old, and there's been nothing since."

"The captain took a risk to even send it," Vayne mused.

"And we may have given the Outriders a hint we can ill afford, should they track it," Leric pointed out. "But it apparently seemed worth the hazard. There is more here than meets the eye."

"Take us through the Geer Falls, with all possible speed," Vayne instructed without commenting on his exec's assessment. "And tell me everything you learned to date about my chosen, before we make our plans."

****

Neira was asleep again when he let himself into his cabin. Already he knew the slight noises she made in slumber and his hearts ached with tenderness before the surge of protectiveness pushed him to sit beside her. He'd spent considerable time in the exercise room after she'd refused him, working his body hard on both the weights and resistance machines. Not accustomed to being denied—or thwarted—it had taken all of his control to leave her and adhere to Shadalla customs, rather than prove to her then and there that they were meant for one another. He had total faith in his ability to seduce her but forced himself to respect the holding period. The exercise room still held her scent, and the memory of her supple body under his own as he took her down during their sparring tended to undermine his efforts.

His pheromones, produced in much higher quantity for his chosen, were already having an effect on her, despite her harsh rejection. He suspected she fought another, very different battle, and he was caught in the fallout of her shored up defenses. She was very well defended, indeed.

The Shadalla had evolved far past their ancestors and their hated cousins, features becoming more humanoid as they left behind many of their animalistic proclivities, and as qualities of mercy and empathy developed in their race. It made them better fighters and conquerors, able to form alliances with other worlds instead of grinding them beneath boot heels, raping and pillaging like the Juxtant. But they were still predators on the battlefield and when it came to seeking and securing a mate, hence the holding period. It kept Shadalla males' beasts in check as they wooed and made their chosen mate both dependent and thoroughly attached before the passion was unleashed on them. But by the great gods it was trying his patience.

To his knowledge, no female withstood a mate past the thirty days of holding, most conceding in the first week. Vayne grimaced. Was it fitting that as a royal he would be forced to wait and prove his restraint as a so-called better man by the nature of his bloodline? He refused to entertain the thought Neira could withstand him and he'd lose her. Thirty days counting down.

Peering down at her in the dim lighting, he studied her features, the usual no-nonsense set of her mouth now relaxed and sweet above that firm chin. He longed to trace the pert slant of her nose and along her high cheekbones, nearly hidden by the sweep of long, dark lashes. Neira Grekov. Russian descent, according to the history files, and had she been born a few centuries ago, likely the daughter of an influential Russian aristocrat. Now a soldier. Ex-soldier, he reminded himself. And perhaps not truly discharged. Leric had also suggested she might be a spy, craftily planted aboard the *Astris*, but Vayne now knew differently. His intuition never failed him, despite his earlier musings.

He hoped to encourage her to grow her silky hair long, although in truth she would come to deny him nothing in time. It was the nature of their kind to mate, then for the female to choose only what her male would prefer, to please with compliance and submission. The idea was vaguely unpalatable, and he squinted in response, then pushed the discomfort away. Events would continue to unfold as they had done for eons, and not even the sovereign could change that. Females were even more valuable now, so highly prized, and it was both necessity and tradition to protect them, hence the manner in which the joining worked. Total submission and surrender was inevitable. *And you absorbed Asula until absolutely nothing remained of her and she faded from you. Perhaps her only, but final, act of defiance.*

Vayne stood abruptly and flexed his shoulders. Asula was different from Neira. Their joining had been politically optimum despite his lack of interest in her, and the fact was she wasn't suitable for someone so strong-willed as him. She would not have faded had she been matched with another, and in truth the hormonal response to make her his chosen had been intentionally manipulated by the scientists. Thinking to fool nature. He ground his teeth when he considered how many such matches had turned out, and mentally he cursed the Home World and its genetic weapon that drove the Shadalla to such measures. He could identify with Neira's rage over feeling powerless. Well, that couldn't be helped.

She was awake now, responding to his angst, her breathing light and quick. He told himself it wasn't only her training that made her open her eyes, but that she *felt* him, for he could move quieter than a whisper.

"We must talk, little warrior."

"About?"

How he regretted the caution coloring her tone. Calling for more light, he waited as the computer adjusted the settings, then retrieved the chair he had sat on earlier. He debated about releasing Neira but had no way of knowing how she would react. Thinking it better that he be able to closely examine her expressions rather than guard against attack, he urged her to sit sideways, using the slack in the tether to lower her hands to her lap. She blinked at him before donning that aloof warrior mask, but she didn't resist when he tucked the cover around her shoulders.

"I will tell you what I have learned and ask that you not prevaricate. There are twelve other females on this ship who assume the same risk. And no, it is not I, not the Shadalla who threaten."

The blood drained from her face and her eyes widened before she gave him one of those nods he expected to become quite familiar with. Vids he'd viewed of her heritage flashed in his brain and he suppressed a smile at the thought of her in furs and diamonds, looking imperiously at her subjects. How he wished this conversation wasn't necessary, because he sensed a dreadful outcome.

"You are Neira Grekov, formerly of the Orion Marines, a sergeant, broken from the rank of captain for reasons I haven't yet been able to determine. You were missing in action nearly two years ago toward the end of the suppression of the Juxtant, in one of the final land battles on Mars. You were rescued by chance on Zores, returned home and honorably discharged. There is no record of you leaving the Home World on the *Astris*, but rather a Neira Graheme, bound for one of the mining planets in the outer quadrant."

Her face was like stone, amazing eyes blank but for the dilated pupils, her lips nearly white. Those lips parted and she clearly forced a response past them. "That is accurate."

"Except for what it doesn't say."

"I don't know what you mean."

"Neira. Little warrior. We are being pursued, or at the very least, hunted. And not because of some replaceable cargo."

"You robbed a passenger ship," she pointed out, but there was no inflection in her tone. Vayne was reminded again of a *leicat*, although he doubted even the feline could hold so steady and immobile in the face of him.

"Don't dissemble." He made sure his voice snapped authoritatively, and she flinched infinitesimally. "Must I ask why you are being sought?"

"Me?" Her color was a bit better, a faint flush stroking her cheeks, and her mouth was nearly that rich red again. "That makes no sense."

He stared into her eyes, and she met him glare for glare. So perhaps she didn't know, the confusion reflected earlier in the tawny depths replaced with stark truth. His recital of her dossier had badly upset her, though, and it was something he'd have to explore later, for he sensed it was the key to her ability to continue to refuse him.

"It might make no sense, but yours was the only file stored on the *Astris* that lacked information. The rest read like an open book. And there is the matter of you traveling under a different name."

She tilted her head and he knew she was working

it through. "I wanted anonymity. After the media coverage. So the captain agreed to modify things a little. I answered to Neira, and I doubt anyone inquired after my other name. So perhaps there is someone else they want, hiding in plain sight. The files on the *Astris* are only as complete as the people who programmed them. And because of my former…profession, it wouldn't surprise me that the information was frugal."

Everything she said made sense and he wished for it to be true. "Do you know the other women on board?"

"Not well. Vicky. The other two not at all. There was another woman. Toya." She stopped speaking and her eyes narrowed.

"Neira?"

"She escaped on a pod. I saw her go."

"The pirate ship has her."

"Then perhaps it's about her, or one of the others on board here."

"What is there about her that bothers you?"

Shrugging, she obviously formulated an answer, but he watched her closely. Neira was cudgeling her memory, not building a lie. "She was in everybody's business and wanted me to take an escape pod with her. She was most insistent and then she broke and ran. It didn't fit with what I knew of her. But then I've lost so many of my skills I could easily be wrong."

Reflecting on how she'd held large men at bay, he doubted it, but she was referring to her assessment skills, he thought. "She was the one who told the pirate captain about you."

"I still don't understand. You mean you knew all of this—from the pirates?"

He shook his head. "Only the bare bones. But you were the only one she could think of who might be worth the time and effort of nine Outriders jumping in hot pursuit of the pirates."

"She might be painting a false trail."

With his recollection of Captain Ristos, he had reservations. The man would have no difficulty eliciting information, even if he suspected the man wouldn't have had to employ time-honored tactics. Not with a woman. Neira read his expression of doubt.

"I assure you, Sovereign. My former employer was thrilled to see the last of me." There was no mistaking the bitter satisfaction in her voice, and he stayed quiet.

****

She thought she would pass out when confronted with a synopsis of her life by the last person—alien—she could have imagined would possess that information. Just how much of a data base did the Shadalla have? He said he knew Earth history, and his turns of phrase, as well as use of slang, was dead-on, if sometimes quite dated, but still… And he was still looking at her, into her, as though determined to pull out all her secrets. But the Outriders weren't looking for her. She had nothing anyone wanted, knew nothing. If the military honored their promise and left her alone—her thoughts staggered to a dead halt. The sovereign didn't know how she'd obtained her discharge, and he'd had one thing wrong.

"What is it, Neira?" There was urgency in his tone, but it was also gentle and caressed her senses.

Maybe the part about the discharge didn't matter. Alexi was a nobody, unless his execution could be fanned to a flame and incite the public. But the other… "I wasn't rescued on Zores." The words escaped despite her. She *needed* to tell him, couldn't fight it any longer.

"The Juxtant's allies didn't have you?" he asked, awareness darkening his handsome face.

"No," she whispered, again unable to lie to him.

"Alexi—Petrov and I were found by a raiding party on Ureses. Quite accidentally when a shield collapsed and they stumbled on the...lair."

The room tilted crazily as the last of her barriers tumbled down like that shield. They were undermined by this alien's intensity, her body's attraction to him and the sense of something far bigger than her, encroaching to swallow her whole. She'd been clinging to control since being brought on board and no longer had the strength to hold on. Her entire being told her to let him take the burden.

She could hear him faintly over the roaring in her ears, calling out her name, then a fumbling at her hands as she keeled over sideways. All that time learning to forget drained away, and she allowed the darkness filled with memories to sweep her under.

"So, the soldier bitch continues to resist, Modeed?" The whining voice of Somar pierced through the pain and Neira tensed despite herself. She'd long since learned that any response drew more unwelcome attention.

"She does," agreed Modeed, her very own private torturer nodding at his superior. *"Although at this stage of the war I doubt whatever she holds will be helpful, sir."*

"You are probably right. We have retreated to our last line, and we'll be taking off within hours. The Zorians will cover our retreat. The Shadalla have come to bolster Earth forces and we all know what that means." Somar made an unpleasant barking sound as he casually ran his long nails up her exposed flank. She could feel the flesh score and part beneath the razor sharp edges. *"Bring this one, and the willowy male. They will provide many hours of amusement. Kill the others."*

The futile lunge against the shackles, an attempt

to get her hands around Somar's throat and squeeze until his pupilless eyes popped, earned her another burst of agonizing energy from the devices attached to her temples. She'd bitten her lips bloody to prevent her screams—and any sharing of the updated battle plans— but a cry of pain escaped this time before Modeed shut it off. He hovered, waiting for her scrambled mind to recover before he acted on his orders, ever the sadist.

No amount of disparaging self-talk kept her eyes open as he went from table to table, dispatching— murdering—the other prisoners, all men and women under her immediate command. Nineteen of them, all her responsibility. She couldn't close off her ears, however, and the horrible sounds of their deaths imprinted in her brain, already addled by the torture. The stench made her gorge rise, and it was only Modeed's precipitous return that unfortunately saved her. He'd turned her enough in the restraints that she didn't choke to death on her own vomit, and that was the cruelest torture of all.

Waking up in a light and airy room several lifetimes later, dressed in clean clothing, her hair washed and her body healed and cleansed, had instilled some kind of curious hope. She dared to think she'd been rescued, but then sank into the depths of hopelessness when she recalled what had transpired in that battle on Mars. And how she'd survived and her troops had not. She'd followed orders this time, having learned her lesson while a captain. It didn't matter that she had possessed firsthand intelligence back then, and disregarded the brass' instructions, winning a strategic choke point on one of Neptune's moons. Free thinking wasn't allowed and she'd been demoted to sergeant. Her troops knew the truth and that had been enough for her— until Mars. Once again the intel had been faulty and she'd led her troops into a trap, back to being a good soldier. They'd acquitted themselves well against the Juxtant and their allies, the Zorians, but in the end over half had died and the rest captured.

She'd explored the space, lost in her memories, berating herself and contemplating the future, when a Juxtant male entered—and turned the bright chamber into the darkest of dark. No...

Her body flooded with energy and was enfolded in warmth. The memories faded. Vayne's scent surrounded her and his deep voice crooned in her ear. "Neira. I have you. It's fine. You're safe."

A part of her wanted to believe him so badly it was a sweet taste in her throat. But he was all tangled up in the reasons she'd fallen back into the past, and it made her struggle desperately to get away, only to wish to weep when he released her. She rolled up against the hull and flattened her back against the unforgiving heft of it. Vayne lifted both arms to show his hands-off stance and the other male with him busied himself packing away what looked like medical supplies.

"You experienced a fugue state, Neira. My medic administered a stimulant and a slow release relaxant now that you've come back to us."

The medic took his leave, and Vayne perched on the far end of the bunk. The position allowed the lighting to throw his features into stark relief, and despite the marked difference in eye color and the existence of a pupil, she saw the similarities. She thought she could credit the relaxant for the fact that her burgeoning scream transformed into a low, anxious moan, but it escaped her nonetheless. Vayne turned his head and gave her a considered glance, and the effects of the lighting vanished, but she knew.

"You're Juxtant." Her comment escaped on a harsh, low whisper past her closing throat and only the drugs kept the terror under a modicum of control.

He went totally rigid, and she saw him press his lips together rather than allow his mouth to drop open in surprise. Then he closed his eyes for a moment, as if impossibly weary. She watched him from the depths of her helplessness, wishing to lose her mind and seek the oblivion of insanity.

Oddly, his quiet, measured response held her together. "No. I'm Shadalla. The Juxtant are cousins, evil animals, and a part of our race no self-respecting Shadalla would acknowledge or accept. Long since separate. Eons separate. We allied with the Home World because of the threat, if you recall."

"Or you've found a way to mask who you are." There was accusation and hatred in her voice and she made no attempt to hide them. Somehow she'd found some resolve, her mind ticking over the possibilities.

****

Vayne marveled at her strength. Neira had clearly experienced a flashback, perhaps a multitude of flashbacks of her unmentionable time as a Juxtant prisoner. She thought he was one of that evil spawn in disguise and was even now standing up to him. His desire and need to protect and possess her nearly overcame the immediate, his cock so hard and aching he felt lightheaded. He could give her such pleasure, replace those terrible memories…but it wasn't yet time. Only his rage at what she had to have experienced as a captive of those monsters steadied his mind and kept him on track.

"We evolved and they didn't. We could have destroyed your world and others, but we chose not to do so. We don't commit atrocities and as you must know, offer honorable work to those looking. We don't take slaves anymore."

"You steal women."

Fuck, it was back to that again. A sticking point for certain, but what else was he to do? "For very good reason. We cannot become extinct."

She pushed harder on the sensitive subject between them. "So why not approach the Home World? Make the offer to Earth's women just as you offer work to the men?"

"To do that would reveal our vulnerability, Neira. Think on that. Who created our issue in the first place? And if they aren't aware of the success of their weapon, it wouldn't be prudent to hand them the information! We are uneasy allies."

Passing a slender hand over her eyes, she murmured, "Hell, I don't know." She dropped her hand and looked up at him. "Do you think they won't figure it out if you keep relieving ships of the female passengers? All of a certain age?"

He waited patiently, and she worked it through. "Oh. That's why you use pirates. The Home World will think the women were sold all over the quadrant. It'll play a few times and then what?"

"Then I'll figure something else out."

She didn't give him anything further, and her body language remained the same. He decided to share additional information, hoping she would offer more. He still suspected she was the reason for the Outrider search. "I'll supply some history on the Juxtant, if you like."

"I don't like. In fact I'll thank you to quit talking about them."

"You are calm with the medication in your system, Neira. It has taken full effect." That and she was borrowing his strength, whether she understood that or not. It was his honor to share with her. "We should use the clarity."

"Why? So you can find a way to evade pursuit?"

"Do you believe your fellow humans' attempt is honorable, little warrior? Do you really want them to catch up with us and take you back?"

That gave her pause. He saw her quick mind consider it.

"No. It won't be honorable. They killed Alexi, you know. My superiors. The public weren't aware of him, so they didn't waste time rehabilitating him." Her voice had taken on a pensive quality.

"Who is Petrov? And this Alexi?" he asked, modulating his voice, trying not to react to his chosen being *rehabilitated*. He could imagine the additional horrors she'd experienced, and at some point had to hear about them. He would take all her pain unto himself, and the sooner the better.

With a twisted smile, she answered. "One and the same. One of my troopers. The only other soldier Somar ordered transported, besides me, from Mars. To Ureses. I thought of him as Alexi—until Ureses. Then it was easier to call him by his last name. Distance us."

"*Somar*." Vayne could taste the other man's foul stench as if he were in the room. Somar the Procurer. It was surely inappropriate to feel relief that this Petrov who figured so often was but one of her troopers. Now deceased. Although she clearly still felt responsible for him, part of her quality of command.

"Do you know Somar?" Suspicion laced her tone again.

"I do. Personally and by reputation. He pretends to be a great warrior, when in truth he procures things— and people—for his master. Ba—"

Her sudden lunge nearly caught him off guard, but he didn't have to defend against the press of her fingers against his mouth. "Shh. Don't say his name. He'll hear you."

His chosen's eyes were filled with terrible fear and madness. The pupils were so wide the surrounding gold of the iris was but a thin outline, shimmering eerily against the black. Vayne wrapped her quivering body up, tucking her head under his chin to hold her against him, blessing the drug the medic had administered. He had no doubt Neira had been triggered and broken down into her past and only the medication held her together. He felt her lapse once again into unconsciousness, but this time it was controlled and healing as he poured his certitude and care past all her desperate, crumbling defenses.

For now he knew. She'd been procured for Baraith, the Monarch of the Juxtants, snatched from the field of battle and, instead of being killed, was transported with all the other spoils of that war into the clutches of the worst Juxtant in their long history. Vayne didn't believe in coincidence, but fate was a different matter entirely. Once again the skeins had been spun to bind all the loose ends together. For surely Neira's connection with Baraith was but another step toward apprehending that monster.

Baraith, who was no longer on Ureses but holed up somewhere else, stripped of his wealth and power. He had only a few followers, most of them scattered throughout the quadrant. Vayne's own hunters were systematically tracking them down and disposing of them, but no one knew where Baraith was, or they weren't telling. The source of the precise marks on the back of Neira's body was now explained, and he wondered that the rest of her was unblemished. Not that it mattered. It had been her spirit and determination that drew him, and her austere beauty, her body virtually invisible beneath the shapeless, black clothing she'd worn at the time.

Meantime, he fervently hoped once her trauma

was purged, that spirit would again present itself and refused to think that it wouldn't. *But you want her for your own, for her to join with you and lose herself once again. How does that make you any different?* He *was* different, he assured himself. He had chosen Neira because of his reaction to her, beyond physical attraction. Chosen her according to Shadalla ancient proclamations and hadn't had her procured for him, or assigned politically with genetic manipulation. Perhaps he'd procured her himself, but if she hadn't been his chosen she would have become his concubine, or be sequestered with the others, awaiting further opportunities on Nibiru.

Even the thought of another male choosing her, sharing a holding period with her, enraged him. Her body responded to his strong emotion with a faint shudder. Immediately, he calmed himself and applied his formidable intellect and logic to their situation. They were now into the Falls and shielded from any pursuit as effectively as if they'd thrown up a shadow field. But at some point they would have to cross open space to his planet and if the Outriders had reason to believe the Shadalla were involved in the looting of the *Astris*, they could be waiting. It had been a mistake for the pirate captain not to destroy that pod.

Carefully placing Neira on the bunk, he covered her again and lay beside her, relishing the position. As sovereign he never had to deny himself a woman's body, especially during his travels unless it was of his own choosing, but this feeling of protecting her, nourishing her with his presence, was entirely satisfying. Well, perhaps not entirely. He needed to join with her, to sink deep into her welcoming, slick heat and give her his seed. She would beg for it, as he'd told her, for there was no other choice, but perhaps she might not shutter her mind against him. The thought of Neira being unable to deny her physical will yet refusing him her heart was a lance to his own. At some point in their brief time together, past the brain chemistry that proclaimed her as chosen, this woman had vanquished him, and no position, no bloodline, was defense against her.

After considering any number of variables and considerations, supplemented by additional information Leric compiled and sent to him, Vayne came up with the most likely explanation. When Neira awoke and partook of a meal, he would discuss it with her. She would receive additional medication, offered of course, but administered regardless, in her best interest. It was imperative that she be helped to address whatever Baraith had done to her. The holding period was also irrevocably counting down. No quarter was given for any kind of circumstances, which included absolutely no time extensions. As sovereign, he expected to face enormous challenges and to shoulder huge burdens, but once again he wondered about his capabilities when it came to this female.

Chapter Six

It seemed all she did was sleep and eat on this cursed ship. The *Tomodr* was much smaller than the *Astris,* of course, but surely there was more to do than be confined to the cabin, sleep and eat. Aside from that one sparring match and the meal with the others she hadn't left these quarters. Neira preferred not to think about the reasons she'd been sleeping and avoided at all costs the thought of certain other things she might be doing with her time. Vayne was still feeding her, the intimacy of the act infiltrating her senses, chipping away at her will.

He'd also helped her cleanse, if help was the proper way to describe it. Sure, she had been weak and uncertain on her feet after her stupid breakdown, and probably because of the drugs that medic, Stenlor, had administered, but she still thought she could have looked after herself. And the sovereign conveniently ignored her order about not touching her. She couldn't fault the almost impersonal way he'd washed her body, although the feel of his strong fingers against her scalp nearly made her moan. There was no one else to care for her, as he said, and she pretended not to hear his comment that it was his privilege.

All of her high-minded intentions had seemed to fall by the wayside, and she'd become a new poster child: Miss Pushover. Lurking behind her muddled thinking, a bogeyman with razor sharp teeth and curved claws waited to spring, but it was held at bay in Vayne's presence, her lack of control somehow less of a concern. It made no sense, because it was the sovereign's insertion into her life that initially chiseled away at her walls… She wasn't tracking well at the moment. They were still in his quarters, and Vayne was watching her pretend to get more comfortably seated.

"We need to have a discussion, little warrior." He wasn't giving her a choice. Oh, his tone was gentle, even compassionate, but implacable. Those strong, handsome features, that level stare, made her want to tell him everything. And lately she felt like his little warrior.

"Why were you banned from the Home World?" Where had that come from? Maybe the drugs were unlocking some of those elusive memories associated with Vayne and the Shadalla.

A sparkle of amusement shone in his turquoise eyes and a corner of that sensuous mouth quirked up. "So you knew of that."

"Just remembered." Like she now recalled more about why the troops called him His Lordship with something like awe and a hint of reverence. It had been before her time, which made this alien considerably older than her, but the war stories tended to live on through the generations. His troops literally laid their lives down for him and he never squandered them. Never. So unlike her superiors.

Vayne reached out and ran a fingertip down her cheek. Neira didn't flinch away. She barely managed not to press into his touch and suppressed a shiver of longing.

"It was during the treaty negotiations. I overstepped my…boundaries."

She waited, insatiably curious, yet not wanting to show it. She could feel the heat of his body. It rolled from him in waves despite the barrier of his uniform, and she well knew how warm and protected he made her feel when he divested himself of his garments. *Protected!* What the hell was going on? He *took* her, *kidnapped* her and wasn't going to let her go. She struggled to put her situation back into perspective and resist whatever impact he was having on her.

Lifting a shoulder, he smiled fully. "There was an ambassador's daughter."

The rush of emotion enveloping her insides and cooling her skin was unmistakable, if not terribly familiar. It was insane to feel such intense jealousy. He meant nothing to her that way, and they both had pasts. The convoluted thinking didn't escape her, and Neira swallowed any words that came boiling up her throat, contenting herself with a raised eyebrow and set lips. Something else niggled but was quashed by her jealous response.

"It was a long time ago, Neira. I was arrogant and held the belief that all women were my right. And it served a political purpose. I was compiling information."

Had he recognized her reaction for what it was? Neira gritted her teeth, noting he'd called her by name, trying to ignore what felt like a bridge to heal her furious rejection of him. Confusion and annoyance surfaced and she managed to address him. "I don't see how anything has changed."

A burst of startled laughter escaped him before he clearly shut it down and narrowed his eyes. "I find myself torn between appreciating your feistiness and the need to remind you of the issue of respect."

"Perhaps the truth stings, Sovereign."

Another laugh, and she badly wanted to smile back. "Like many Shadalla who fought in the wars, I availed myself of the females. Not by force, ever, and there were no offspring from those unions because we were at war. I wouldn't leave any innocents to face that. I can't change what happened then, but I assure you, little warrior, you are my last woman. And if that sounds arrogant, I still stand by it."

"And I told you—"

"I know what you told me. I well remember. I

can't say that I've ever been rejected before, and to be rejected by one's lifemate…"

She studied him, drawn by both his physique and good looks, and appreciating, despite herself, how he'd opened up and shown some vulnerability. Did she actually have an effect on him? The little hint of power tasted fine, and it wasn't one she wanted to twist to use against him. Her heart kick-started at the thought and she sucked in a deep breath to calm it. Where was her earlier resolve? She should be taking any opportunity to talk him into releasing her from this ridiculous pursuit. She needed to gain her freedom.

"You feel it, Neira. Just as I do, though it's understandable you'll take somewhat longer to come to terms with it. I was anticipating finding you and it came to pass."

"You'll forgive me if I'm skeptical. How long would you have looked?"

"Until I found someone compatible. A chosen. But I am blessed that I didn't have to look past the *Astris*."

This time bitter disappointment flooded over her, washing away all those softer feelings. *Someone.* Not a fairy tale, then. Not one in a million, a billion, chances. She shook her head against the fanciful thought. Stupid. Even as a girl she'd scoffed at fate and true love and all. So allowing even a hint of fancy to impact her was insane and moronic. Vayne could have easily spied *someone compatible* amongst the rest of the women. He still could. And that fine, flowery assurance of her being the last woman would be just another broken promise in her life.

"What convoluted thinking just passed through your mind?"

Ah, now he was being condescending, paternal. Asshole. She forced a smile. "I'm still not interested in being your mate and broodmare."

His sensuous mouth flattened for an instant and his eyes iced over before he visibly collected himself. "Your body tells you—and me—otherwise, little warrior. I take exception to you referring to yourself in a deprecating manner. And you think too much. I expect it's a combination of your military training and what you suffered at the hands of the Juxtant."

The shrug she attempted was spoiled by a shudder and Vayne scooped her up and held her close, his warm breath stirring the hair at her temple.

"Share with me, Neira. The medic will administer whatever medication you require, but this *thing* festers in you."

"I don't talk about it. I had therapy." Her assertion came out muffled against his shoulder and while she knew she should be pulling away from him and keeping her distance, she couldn't do it. She was back to feeling protected and safe.

"We've extracted part of your medical file," Vayne offered, and it gave her the strength to lean away and look at him. He made no apology for being so intrusive into her life and she eased apart to sit farther away than she thought he'd allow.

"How did you get access to my information?"

"Tools of the trade, the secrets of war. We keep our friends close and our enemies closer."

"But, the treaty."

He scoffed. "Your own experience tells you how honorable the old-world leaders actually are. Even the heads of the military have no honor. We will always have evidence of this."

She would have liked to delay further, but resigned herself to dealing with him sooner than later. "So you accessed my file."

He caught up her hand and pressed it between both of his, and she felt her pulse fluttering like a small bird in a living, warm cage. "They tried to erase your memories of captivity, but there was disagreement as to how successful they were. It makes me wonder why they were so desperate to cleanse your mind instead of heal it."

Tugging her hand free, she wrapped both arms around herself in a poor facsimile of a hug and forced her eyes to meet Vayne's. Her breathing almost instantly slowed and her heart rate calmed. He stared back at her with openness and acceptance reflected in those turquoise orbs.

Striving for a calm tone, like the one she used to report to her superiors, she said, "I learned what they did to Petrov. There were certain drugs I couldn't avoid, the ones administered through intravenous, but I didn't always take the others. So while I was sedated and met with any number of shrinks, all provided by the military, I was able to avoid a lot of the heavier stuff."

She didn't add that she had allies amongst the hospital staff, soldiers like herself who did their best to keep her educated and updated as to what was planned for her. They were the ones who smuggled out Alexi's files and information to others who secreted them so she would have leverage to secure her discharge. It had been a delicate balancing act but she'd succeeded, if not without considerable help. Neira hoped her friends and allies remained undiscovered and were safe.

"You were interrogated extensively about your time with…the Juxtant."

Trepidation coiled in her belly and mounted swiftly. She was not thinking about that time. Nor sharing any part of it with him. "I don't recall."

"Neira." Once again it was as though he was

looking straight into her inner self, learning all her secrets. "I suspect you possess something, some piece of knowledge perhaps those on the Home World either wish to obtain, or to keep you from sharing it with others."

Swallowing back an immediate negative response, a literal pain grinding in her head, she considered his supposition. He was basing it on certain facts that didn't necessarily stand up to close scrutiny. The Outriders might be searching for someone else—or the pirate captain had been misled. There were a number of different explanations, and she preferred to believe them, regardless of a swirling sense of dread that Vayne was correct. She shook her head.

"We will keep searching, and it may occur to you."

"I have so much to thank you for, Sovereign," she retorted, sarcasm shoring up her denial. "Kidnapped, my future mapped out in a manner I'd have never entertained, and now you want me to think about a time in my life that…that will tear me apart."

She was nearly whispering toward the end of her attempted rant, and absurd tears welled. She scrubbed at them with the heels of her hands and Vayne wrapped her up again, tucking her head beneath his chin. Breathing in his scent, she settled in his arms and cautiously thought about that first day she'd made Baraith's acquaintance.

"Neira Grekov. Of the Orion Marines. So very few of you left. Two that we know of." The Juxtant was big. Bigger than either Somar or Modeed, even though the vulpine features were the same, the wide, dark eyes with no pupils, soulless and cruel. It was like looking into the abyss. He wore his clothing with casual elegance on his tall, muscular body but she intuited the evil behind his trappings. She kept silent and wished there had been any kind of weapon to be fashioned from the objects in the

room.

"I am Baraith. Monarch Baraith." At her sudden tension, he smiled, sharp teeth gleaming in the available light. "Ah, my reputation precedes me. Well deserved, I assure you. The Juxtant are losing this war, Neira Grekov. I find myself reevaluating my future in the little time I anticipate is left."

"What possible role can I play?" She could have slapped herself for responding.

He'd been on her before she saw him move, a hand shoved into her hair to snag the short strands and yank her head back. His breath was fetid, hot, and she saw the craziness in his eyes. She regretted her offhand comment even more in that moment. She'd been afraid when at Modeed's mercy but interrogation was expected. This was so very different. Modeed had a job to do, a goal to attain. Baraith had no use for her other than as something to use for his amusement, to toy with, break and discard. However long it took.

"You'll entertain me as I make my preparations. Alleviate my boredom." His tiny smirk worried her more than any leer or ignorant comment would have. The casual way he shoved her away underscored how weak and incapable she actually was, worn down by the torture and lack of food and water, not to mention the anguish of losing her troopers. Her cleanliness and fresh clothing was but a thin veneer, and one that had given her false hope, cleverly chosen so this psycho could rip it away.

Baraith sauntered to the door but paused before exiting. "The other Marine? His name is Petrov. I believe the two of you will provide an excellent distraction."

There was no need to relive the memories of the ensuing days. The human body tended to forget the pain inflicted on it, but the mental and emotional aspects were a different matter. If it had only been Neira…but Petrov was part of it and used as a most effective tool to break her down. Alexi Petrov shouldn't have made the Corps with his slender build and girlish good looks, but those very attributes hid a remarkable Marine, tough and resilient, and very talented in combat. But it was his appearance that drew Baraith, and Neira found she'd do anything to save him from that sick bastard's attentions. And Baraith had known it from the beginning. And in the end Petrov wasn't tough or resilient enough.

Letting those memories go, surprised at how she could view them so dispassionately, she answered Vayne. "I don't remember anything that would mean something to the Home World. The time I spent with Baraith didn't exactly involve talking strategy or politics." She sounded matter-of-fact, as though the things that had taken place were…distanced somehow. Like they had happened to someone else. Even her body felt relaxed and under control.

A big hand stroked down her back and up again. Vayne's deep voice rumbled above her. "Was there anyone else there? Besides you and Petrov?"

Flickers of Petrov begging Baraith not to punish her for some imagined infraction on his part teased her mind and she forced them aside, deep sadness coloring the memories as she accepted that she hadn't saved Petrov in the end. Worse, she'd undermined his male ego and natural need to protect the vulnerable—women and children—by negating his sacrifice and asking for the torture instead. Because he was her trooper and she, his sergeant. Time-honored roles that meant nothing in the long run. Tears welled up again and there were too many to brush away. Neira truly wept for the first time in forever, maybe since she was a child, and a part of her wondered that she was comfortable weeping in this alien's arms. He didn't speak again, merely shifted her closer and offered that comfort, his big body supporting her without any discernible effort.

When she thought past the perverted innovations Baraith initiated almost every day, forcing her to pull rank on her trooper to spare him irreparable physical harm, she delved deep and recalled Somar inserting himself into the room on occasion. The monarch had been irritated by the interruption—the alien didn't share his amusements with others—but had settled when his procurer whispered a name or gestured to someone hovering outside the door. Baraith would abandon his twisted play and vanish for hours, sometimes not returning for a few days, giving both Neira and Petrov time to regroup, or pray for release. Alexi had come to hate her in the end…

She was exhausted, sucked dry, and no closer to fulfilling Vayne's speculation. "There wasn't anyone there I recall. Somar was there, and he spoke some names to Baraith but I can't remember them. But whomever it was must have been an equal—or somebody he needed."

"It may come to you," he soothed. "How do you feel?"

"I'm okay. Tired." It was very peculiar. Normally, even traversing the edges of those memories created panic attacks that immobilized her, so she avoided that at all costs. Perhaps it was the medication. *Or maybe it's Vayne.* And maybe it could be any Shadalla who thought her to be his chosen.

"Do you wish to sleep? Or would you care to dress and walk with me?"

"Leave the cabin?" She sounded pathetically hopeful, and it wasn't only to put some distance between them.

His chest rumbled with laughter. "Yes, Neira. I understand how confined you have felt, but I believe you are well enough to move about."

Even though he didn't acknowledge the primary reason she was confined, Neira found she really didn't want to fight with him. Not that she was going to acquiesce and become his lifemate, actually bear his children. A vision of a toddler, big for his age, with Vayne's golden skin and amazing eyes sprang, lifelike, into her mind, and she blinked rapidly to fragment the picture. No. Not Ever. She was going to withstand him, refuse him and lead her own life. The lonely, empty life she'd known to expect after gaining her freedom from the military.

He didn't insist she wear the *paca*. Instead he provided another floor-length shift, the soft material covering her completely, from throat to toes, and a thought occurred. "Is this the normal apparel on Nibiru?"

Vayne's eyes flickered and she braced for a lie. "No. You would be veiled and hooded as well."

"Excuse me?"

"We are evolved, Neira, from the predators we once were, but that doesn't change the fact some of our less disciplined males react…strongly…to females, whether or not they are their chosen. Especially now that there are so few of them. Home World women are particularly appealing, and those of us fortunate enough to have found our brides cherish and protect them."

"Oh, spare me." She remembered hearing of the customs of other cultures on Earth before the blending, and what Vayne shared smacked of fundamentalism with a hefty dash of misogyny. "I'll never hide myself away like that."

"Then you'll remain in my home." Oh, he was acting the boss of her, and it rankled. The idea of being cherished and protected—he'd spoken of that before— burbled in her head like a sweet, refreshing stream on a hot day, but there were too many strings attached.

"You forget I haven't agreed to be your—" She almost said broodmare but realized she was already treading on thin ice. And she really wanted to leave the cabin.

"You haven't, little warrior. But I am hopeful." He didn't look hopeful. He looked as though it was a done deal and so she stuck the needle in.

"Your kind lack self-control."

When he drew himself up and loomed over her, she supposed it should have been intimidating, but his features no longer reminded her of Baraith, and while Vayne could make her captivity uncomfortable, she had absolutely no fear for her safety. Her physical safety. Her emotional well-being was another matter, because damned if she didn't want to retract her little dig.

"Insinuating there are major difference between our species is frivolous, Neira, and a distraction you utilize when you feel threatened. I am certain you don't fear me, so why push so hard? As for self-control, we pride ourselves on possessing that quality." His smooth voice once again covered that underlying steel resolve.

"Then why cover the women?"

"Come. I grow tired of this pointless conversation." He reached to draw her to her feet.

Yanking her arm away, she shook her head. "You either don't trust your brethren or you don't trust your lifemates. I wonder which it is?"

Neira stood without Vayne's help and slipped around him to approach the door. The silence drew out. Then he was behind her, one big hand stretching to authorize the lock to open. He didn't speak as they made their way down the corridor, although he kept her close and she could feel the unsettled emotions rolling off of him. His crew treated him with respect but didn't fawn, and she liked that. He was a natural leader, at least her kind of leader, as the war stories had indicated. She didn't want to approve of him, but it was becoming more and more difficult.

Her outfit was quite comfortable, affording her ease of movement and keeping her warm yet allowing her skin to breathe. The idea of having her head and face covered made her sweat a bit, however, and she moved a little quicker at the thought.

"Neira?"

Alarmed at how he picked up on every little nuance, even away from the confines of his cabin, she pretended not to hear him, craning her neck to feign an interest in one of the display panels.

Slipping an arm around her waist, he tucked her against him as they moved along. "Are you all right?"

"Fine." She smiled and tried not to melt against him. She was so not a *girl*.

The warmth of his breath stirred the longer tendrils of hair on her crown and she was again reminded of how big he was, despite her own above-average height—for the women of her species. "How tall are Shadalla females?"

Vayne halted in his tracks and she stuttered to one beside him, having no choice, given his hold on her. He looked down at her and lifted a brow. "Perhaps two handsbreadth taller than you, and they are even more athletic. As a rule they are heavier with larger breasts and rounder…hips. And aside from a lack of body hair, Earth and Shadalla females are alike in their genital anatomy."

TMI. Neira didn't care to think about what he preferred. She was comfortable with her sparse landing strip of curls, close cropped out of habit, like the hair on her head. Keeping clean on the battlefield wasn't the easiest thing, and soldiers had enough to worry about without personal hygiene being an issue. So she merely nodded to indicate she'd heard the information and decided not to ask anything more along those lines. Besides, it felt ever more intimate, talking and sharing with her captor. *Your husband. Your lifemate.* She struggled against the little voice.

Noting how the crew observed her was next on her list of things to do, anxious to determine if she might truly be in need of protection. The big males did indeed cast their gazes over her, thoroughly and with great interest, but she detected no hint of salacious intent from any of them. And Neira was a master at recognizing such things. There was, perhaps, regret in their regard and even envy. That, she could understand, considering the dearth of available Shadalla females, and no doubt all women would garner looks and appraisal, but there was nothing disrespectful she could detect. Armed with her observations, Neira was going to pursue her earlier challenge with the sovereign at another time.

Vayne steered her in the crew's mess and helped her into a chair. It should have grated against her independent spirit, but that part was taking a vacation, because the rest of her appreciated his chivalry—and wanted to preen in the face of it. Had she always had this need to be cared for so solicitously? *Cherished*, Vayne called it. There had never been the opportunity so perhaps he was awakening it.

"I will bring refreshment."

Neira watched him stride toward the galley and appreciated his fine form. She found herself smiling, something she did so rarely even before her time on Ureses. Her body had been aware of him since the beginning and totally stirred to life that first time she'd seen him naked and erect, hard for her. But since then she'd been simmering, like a pot on the stove, ready and waiting for whatever flavor of the day required its contents. Her emotional instability had taken precedence earlier, allowed her to manage and sometimes ignore the sensuality Vayne effortlessly oozed for the most part, but now her arousal was boiling over. Her breasts weighed heavier, the nipples pricking into tight nubs, and the saddle between her thighs, all plump folds and slick juices, couldn't be ignored. Yet ignore it she must, because she understood there would be no quick fuck, no mutual satisfaction of primal urges with Lord Vayne Palldyn, Sovereign of the Southern Range, planet Nibiru. Unrequited lust shouldn't make the middle of her chest ache, and she rubbed at it surreptitiously, shifting her weight to squeeze her legs together.

The last time she'd had sex was maybe a month before that last battle, a long time ago for many, but Neira hadn't had even the slightest urge to pleasure herself, let alone seek out a partner since being rescued. The time in therapy had equally doused any thought of sexual intimacy…and the memories that leaked past the drugs had stomped anything rising from the ashes of her butchered libido, flat.

She spied Vicky a few tables over, with the Shadalla officer who had apparently believed her to be his chosen, and thought to go and speak with the young woman, but the pair were clearly having a moment. It was almost sickeningly sweet, and most certainly sappy, the way Vicky gazed up at Leric, her tilted head resting on his shoulder, his arm wrapped snugly around her. Neira could almost taste the hormones wafting through the air and found them unpalatable. Her arousal dimmed and her belly clenched. Vicky appeared…under the influence, altered.

"*Valki* and a light pastry, Neira." Vayne set the food in front of her and she started, tearing her gaze away from the couple.

"Thank you," she said automatically as he settled next to her, the heat of his body so damn evident.

When she reached for the ale, Vayne caught her hand. "My privilege, little warrior."

He talked about his home planet as he fed her bites of the pastry, something with a filling she didn't recognize, in between sips of the *valki*. Crew members marched in and out, some taking food with them, others sitting at a respectful distance from their table. They continued to give her and Vayne looks, but again Neira found nothing intolerable, and it was probably her imagination that more and more of them began to file in. She didn't see Sheera or Alondra and planned to ask after them.

"I see Vicky and her...and Leric."

Vayne glanced over and she could have sworn he purred. For sure it was a sound in his chest that was remarkably like the one the base cat made when anyone scratched its ears. She wondered what happened to old Scruffy.

"Their bonding is complete," he said, satisfaction evident in his voice. He stared at her for a moment and she felt wanting somehow, like there'd been a competition and she'd lost.

"They do look like an Earth couple. All swoony and all over one another. Like on a honeymoon."

His brow furrowed, then cleared. "Ah, you refer to the time after the wedding."

"Yes."

Leric abruptly stood and gathered Vicky into his arms, carrying her out of the mess with what seemed like indecent haste. She could have sworn every male in the room moaned under their breath and her sexual interest in Vayne revved back up. She tamped it down—hard—

thinking of the cold nights on Neptune and the frozen waterscape of Mars.

"Not a honeymoon," he said. "That is the state of their connection for the rest of their time together, Neira, though they will not flaunt it once they've adjusted."

She scoffed and tried not to let Vicky's capitulation feel as though Neira had ordered the young woman to offer herself up. "Right. Like that intensity lasts."

Pressing closer, Vayne lowered his head. "It lasts. As you will discover."

Inching away, Neira shook her head. "I'll never get that…clingy. It's not me."

She felt him sigh. "Neira. It's not a bad thing. It's the Shadalla way and our mates have no reason nor inclination to complain, or wish it any other way."

There was something she didn't understand here and it was ginormous. "I'd like you to explain what you mean by that." Again, suspicion surged. "Was Victoria drugged?"

"Let's adjourn to our quarters. I'll explain—"

"No. Tell me here. Unless it's a secret from the crew? Like their inability to *control* themselves?"

His features hardened and the turquoise in his eyes darkened to shards of dark blue. His lips pressed into a straight line. She'd kept her voice down but even so knew challenging this man, showing disrespect, was something he didn't tolerate. But fuck if she cared. She knew whatever he had to say—supposing he told the truth—was pivotal in whatever was going on.

****

Do or die. Another Home World euphemism. Well, death wouldn't be the issue, but it might feel like it. His little warrior was calling him out. Shadalla females were taught the process before it ever came to being

117

chosen. Vayne readily admitted that certain shortcuts were taken when it came to Earth females, because it stood to reason the hurried courtships might have been hampered had they been apprised of Shadalla males' abilities to sweep aside any opposition. It was not rape, not at all. But it wasn't totally aboveboard. More like enhanced seduction, because there was no resisting it. *Except your little warrior is doing just that.* He was angry with her for pushing him but angrier at himself for thinking he might have avoided this conversation. Perhaps having the holding period on the *Tomodr* wasn't his best choice, although it had worked extremely well for Leric. And he was still trying to find a way out of this instead of answering her.

"I told you of the chemistry. That which tells us males we have found a chosen. We then involuntarily create and emit pheromones, similar to those humans secrete to entice a mate, albeit in larger, more intense quantities. Because the female is a chosen, she is receptive to these pheromones and..." Vayne stalled out, wondering how best to frame what he had to say. "She embraces the attraction and accepts. She ultimately surrenders her will and becomes part of her mate."

Neira's golden eyes glowed with outrage before she narrowed them. "I don't pretend to understand the science behind attraction, Palldyn. I do know that Earth women tend to do stupid and impetuous things when they become infatuated with someone. It sounds like the same thing."

He shook his head and kept his eyes locked with hers. "There is nothing stupid or impetuous about it, Neira. It is a natural process."

"It sounds like being drugged," she muttered. "And does the male become part of the female?"

By the gods of Isord. He should have insisted on

having this conversation in his quarters, for he well knew the crew were hanging on his every word, their hearing far superior than his little warrior knew. But he knew he must be honest and omit nothing, despite how it might send their bonding awry. "No."

She was on her feet, balanced in a familiar stance—fight or flight—and it was only with considerable control that Vayne remained seated and relaxed, refusing to provoke her. Their audience of over half his fucking crew was abnormally quiet, perhaps holding their breath. Who the hell was manning his ship? He focused on Neira.

"I lost myself once, Sovereign. In fact I doubt I recovered all I was. I'm not doing it again, pheromones be damned, so that you can do your part to repopulate your planet. And I'm pretty sure the other women you stole would have an opinion if given the information you just shared."

"We are desperate, Neira, to ensure the continuation of our species. I grant you that. But a Shadalla male is not complete until he is bonded."

"Excuse me? You all seem to have it together. You're a species that pretty much rules the galaxy, after all."

Gesturing to the crew, who were now sitting, to a man, at rigid attention, their eyes trained directly on him, Vayne spoke. He told his little *leicat* the final piece of information that, if widely known, could spell the end of his race. "We face a double-edged sword, little warrior. Our females are nearly extinct or barren, as I told you. But without a lifemate the male Shadalla fade."

She didn't relax much, but her head tilted and he watched her process. She scanned the other males before returning her gaze to him. Her smooth, high brow furrowed. "You—all of you—will die if you don't bond?

But we all die. Are you saying a lifemate makes you immortal?"

"We live at least three hundred of your Earth years if bonded. Fifty, if not. Even those of royal blood. You could say we have considerable impetus to bond and procreate."

"But you have to be far older than fifty. History…the war…you were in the forefront back then. How do you explain that?" Neira obviously thought she'd caught him out in a lie, and she edged backward.

"I was bonded once before."

Her full lips parted for a moment and her eyes widened before she collected herself, and her emotions were hidden from the crew. Vayne felt them, though, and they were both a stroke and a slap to his ego. Neira struggled with stark jealousy, followed by suspicion and disdain. "Where is she?"

"She faded. It was a genetically manipulated bond and she was unable to maintain it."

A brief beat of silence. "I'm sorry for your loss."

Vayne was overwhelmed by the sadness now emanating from his bride, any hint of the wild *leicat* quelled. Neira felt for him, assumed his heart had been broken, and he had no idea how he was going to reassure her without harming his case. Asula was but a faint memory, a regret, and while he honored her, there was nothing about her that detracted from his need for Neira. Because what they had hadn't been real. He took heart that Neira felt enough for him to experience jealousy and concern. Their physical attraction wasn't in doubt, but he required her trust, and, as he'd come to accept, her heart.

Acknowledging her condolences with a grave nod, he took advantage of her softening demeanor and rose, once again grasping her arm to escort her. There was a collective sigh behind them, and he knew that the conversation would be repeated throughout the ship within moments. Taking another calculated risk, he turned toward the lift. Neira might appreciate the sights and sounds of the bridge, and he would continue to show he was putting his trust in her. Perhaps there was a different path.

As they made their way, she looked at him, her features pensive. "Why isn't Vicky veiled? Because it's not about risk to her, is it?"

"You won't see her again during our travels, Neira. Nor will the rest of the crew, despite how disciplined they are. It's too painful a reminder for them, how short their lifespan might well be, especially when there are no young to replace them and there is so much to be accomplished. And in truth, on Nibiru some have acted out toward a chosen, out of their minds with pain and desperation. We are not *that* evolved. So covering our lifemates in public is kinder for all, and safer. Victoria will now exude such joy and contentment that it will be vastly uncomfortable for males to be around her."

"So you need another lifemate to live another century or so."

Vayne sucked in air against the truth, more than a figurative blow. It was true, yet it wasn't. "My deceased bride somehow extended my lifeline. The genetic manipulation was successful in that regard. And it is true that you will extend it further. Neira, I have responsibilities. I require heirs. That too is a duty. But I also want a bride."

"And I just happened to—" The doors slid open to display the bridge and Neira bit back whatever she was about to say. He reached out to soak up her emotions and tasted resignation flavored with bitterness.

"Sovereign!" Jurlek distracted him with his worried tone. "I was about to contact you. We have plotted a number of vessels on a direct trajectory between Nibiru and the end of the Falls. No confirmed identification yet, but we suspect Home World ships. There are nine in total."

Neira stiffened beside him but remained silent, and Vayne thought quickly. "How long before you are certain?"

"Seven hundred twenty stints."

Much of their force was scattered around the galaxy, and he quickly calculated how many he'd willingly spare from the defense of Nibiru in the event the Home World had devious plans. "Send a coded message to command. Request three ships to rendezvous via a circuitous route. Hold here."

His navigator nodded but in the exec's absence spoke as Leric would, alerting his commander to all possibilities. "The message may be tracked."

"Agreed. Send a probe and have it relay the message obliquely. And then we wait." The *Tomodr* would definitely require the support of additional ships, because there was something intrinsically nasty afoot. But he also wouldn't risk his planet. Vayne didn't respect the treaty after all, if for essential reasons, and he wasn't a total hypocrite.

This time offering Neira his arm, he was gratified when she took it and allowed him to lead her from the bridge, as elegant and controlled as any indigenous royal lifemate. She said nothing the entire way back to his quarters—their quarters—and he hoped they had the time for what he needed to do. It meant less time to answer all the questions and concerns she was certain to raise about her ordained role.

Chapter Seven

The walk back to the confines of Vayne's cabin passed in a blur. Too much information once again, only this time it didn't impact the same way. Neira was torn between worry over why the Home World had vessels lying in wait for her—and unless they were after the Shadalla, having somehow found out their part in the sacking of the *Astris*, she had to accept the odds were high the hunt was on for *her*. It made no sense unless she indeed held vital information in the depths of her psyche. The idea made her nauseous, because the future absolutely didn't bode well.

"You understand we've run out of options." Vayne allowed the door to slide closed before he spoke.

"You think that I have a piece to an important puzzle."

Gesturing her to sit on the bunk, Vayne crossed to the far wall and touched the screen to life. She noted how he turned his back to her more and more as though he trusted her not to act out against him. It wasn't the lack of energy, sucked out of her by the turn of events that had triumphed over that urge, either, nor the acceptance of having nowhere to run. She wasn't even so opposed to him touching her in ways different that his caring, protective mien, despite how her independent self protested. It was disconcerting. Her thoughts whirling, she focused on what he was sharing.

"Leric, when he hasn't been furthering his suit with Victoria, has entered all the known data into our computer. I was going to discuss this with you in any event, after you recovered more fully. I know you have other questions that I would hope can wait, at least until we address this issue."

He wasn't avoiding the elephant in the room, and she appreciated it. It wasn't the time and place to talk more about Vicky and how Neira had indeed tossed her right into the maw of sexual servitude. But that independent part of her surged to the fore. Completing Leric be damned. It wasn't their fault that the Home World rulers had done something so heinous, and it simply wasn't fair that Earth's women would have to right that wrong without much say in the matter. Although shit like that seemed to always fall to women.

Maybe the Shadalla would have to accept their lot and learn to adapt. Lots of species across the universe had done so. It was called evolution, or maybe bouncing back after an extinction level event. It didn't matter that it upset her terribly to think Vayne's life could be cut short. He'd already been lucky, if not in love, then with a longer lifespan. He'd just have to go looking for another chosen to extend this one. And if that bothered her nearly as much, then she was being contrary and selfish…and a total girl. That final thought gave her the strength to cease and desist. *She who fights and runs away, lives to fight another day. Old Russian saying.*

Forcing her attention back to the more pressing matter, she stared at the flow chart Leric had compiled. At first the numbers and events meant little to her, for many had taken place a long time ago, and they were nothing she'd read in Earth history that she recalled. As a pattern coalesced, she tore her gaze away and stared at Vayne. A new history lesson had unfolded within that chart and held terrible implications. "No," she breathed.

Neira thought she possessed more than a modicum of intelligence and most certainly had an ability to string words together in coherent ways, but it seemed she had lost the skill to do more than protest when faced with the improbable. Being a chosen. Intended as a royal broodmare. No and no. And finally, *no* to that pattern she interpreted. Her time in the military placed her in the final stages of the war and at the mercy of the Juxtant, one of two Marines to survive and be held by Baraith, Vayne's mortal enemy. She'd boarded the *Astris* only to be kidnapped by Vayne, and she could well hold information he required about the bio weapon because of her imprisonment under Baraith. But clearly there were forces at work here beyond her understanding and perhaps beyond Vayne's. Although he was probably more a believer than she in the whims of fate. Fate. According to the conclusion she'd drawn from the raw data, their lives had always been entwined and the outcome inevitable. Lifemates.

"You see it, then." Was there admiration in his voice? More fool him. She railed against fate. She'd been in the wrong place at the right time was all. Nothing admirable about that, definitely the wrong time for her, and it had left her stunted and damaged. *Not true. He's taken that from you, the pain and trauma. You are more yourself, like the Neira Grekov of old. Right*, she told that unwelcome voice. *And he'll take everything else until I'm but an extension of him, a resource for him to draw from and live a long life.* Neira no longer wished to die, no matter the form of death. Vayne had perhaps healed her soul, given her back her life, but what price would he exact? *Is being part of him—like him—such a terrible thing? Why fight what is meant to be when he's come to mean so much to you?* She quashed that reasonable, inquiring voice playing the devil's advocate. She'd had quite enough of the devil.

"You've been searching for the ones who unleashed the genetic weapon on the Shadalla." She summarized what she'd detected. "And you have evidence it was the Juxtant who provided the necessary scientific information to build such a thing, if not the technology, and the means to deliver it to Nibiru." She drew the heel of one hand over her brow. There were no coincidences, merely actions and reactions, cause and effect that combined, forming patterns and creating outcomes with a common denominator. "And apparently there's an opinion that I know a name—names, because of my time with Baraith, so I'm a threat to the conspirators."

Ah, and now she was minimizing that terrible torture and mind-crippling agony at the mercy of the Juxtant ruler. Her *time* with that psychotic bastard.

The sovereign stared back, unblinking, and she desperately wanted to crawl inside his head and take refuge, because it wasn't minimization. She had indeed found a way to cope and deal—using whatever it was he provided her. The therapies of the Home World had been but a thick bandage between her and the horror. Before she gave in and voiced her epiphanies and her need, a thought struck her. "But the Juxtant attacked the Home World and all its planets. Why help them?"

Shrugging, Vayne answered, "I expect the amount of mistrust on either side led to betrayal. Or perhaps they saw the way the war was turning. More likely, those who gave the orders for genetic homicide were a small faction and acted without the agreement of all. I have located a few already, but regrettably they didn't survive to meet with me and…share the other conspirators' names."

"A small faction. Which is why you didn't hold them all responsible. All humans and their allies." Her grudging respect grew.

"We don't destroy the innocent, Neira. We pride ourselves on seeing the forest for the trees, as your species has said. I only wish to find those remaining monsters responsible. Those still alive." He spoke with no inflection, and his assertion was more powerful as a result. It left no doubt as to the fate of those people.

"The computer suggests a scenario that one or all of those individuals is aware of my…time with Baraith, and were in touch with him while I was there. They are concerned about what I might know." She figured she might as well sum it up. "That explains the in-depth probing by the military of my time in captivity, then. Although not the efforts to help me suppress the trauma."

"Perhaps they believed if you couldn't recall anything of significance despite their efforts, then ensuring you kept it buried was in their best interests. But it would have worked at cross purposes. They weren't concerned about your best interest."

It was nothing different than the conclusion she'd come to, and Neira nodded. "Petrov probably knew," she mused, "and it came out. So he was put down. I could have met the same fate if not for my contacts and friends. It was Alexi's death by his own military that granted me escape. They feared I'd out them."

"Politicians and those high up in the military are nothing if not strategists, Neira. Someone called in those favors, and to be fair, your superiors could easily have been misled. Told something along the lines of national security. Soldiers follow orders, especially from politicians."

"As the Shadalla warriors follow yours. But you've been a soldier. And they know this, so obeying you can be done with a clear conscience."

Vayne stilled, and those turquoise eyes filled with wonder as his features softened. "Your understanding is the highest compliment, my love."

They stared at one another while Neira strove to resist the lure of that honesty and the endearment. Vayne blinked and spoiled the moment, to her relief. "One would wonder if you mightn't have met with an accident on the mining colony, if not on the way there."

She stood and paced in the small area, trying to ignore his size and strength, knowing he would hold her close and ease her angst if she allowed it. In fact, she was both surprised and disappointed he hadn't made the attempt. "Toya. Was she a spy? Or my assassin?"

Moving with that eerie quickness and silence, he wrapped her up, ignoring her pathetic attempt to resist. Contrary was her middle name. That, or conflicted. "It is pure conjuncture, little warrior. But it does follow."

When he lifted her and carried her to the bunk, she didn't protest. He made quick work of stripping off her garment and sliding her between the covers. She became aware of how chilled she'd been again, cold to her inner core until Vayne had held her. The warmth was pervasive and she tingled, all thoughts and concerns about what was to come banished, at least for the time being. More of Vayne's doing, no doubt, but she welcomed it.

"You've been so brave for so long, my little warrior. It has distracted you from what you need—and deserve." He slid in beside her, also nude, instructing the lights to dim, and formed a heated bulwark against the universe. "Will you trust me, Neira? To plumb your memories and keep you safe through your recollection?"

She retained enough composure to qualify her response. "On this I'll trust you."

Vayne smiled against her hair, or so it seemed. "Ah, so difficult. All right, agreed. On this."

It might have been a form of hypnosis, and one that would be far better received in certain circles than the more typical approaches. Neira allowed her body to relax against Vayne's and listened to his voice as he suggested, aware her breathing was becoming synchronized to his. Their hearts beat closely, again with a faint echo, like a stutter step, and she meandered down pathways deep in her psyche she never thought—or wanted—to walk again. In spirit-saving safety. All of those horrible hours spent under Baraith's torment unfolded, inch by excruciating inch. Except, held in Vayne's thrall, she viewed it almost dispassionately, if with a certain sadness, as she shared with him. The memories flowed over her, slowing when others entered the room or called Baraith away, individuals close by... She could now pluck out names, and language and even faces, no longer clouded by the agony she and Alexi Petrov shared. The latter memory wrenched her heart sideways, the way she'd failed her trooper.

"Shh. You did your best." Vayne rocked her, and Neira became aware of the tears sliding down her face.

"I know. But Petrov was so young, yet so male. Protective. And our roles—"

"Were reversed. Your position was untenable, Neira. So brave for so long, you needn't carry that burden. I'll take it from you—there is no need for you to strain beneath it, be forever in control," he crooned.

Oh, how she wanted to believe him and find the courage to seek more than survival. She'd felt the tears in her psyche knit and heal beneath his benevolence and tender care and anything seemed possible. Vicky's blissful countenance swam behind her closed eyelids and sudden terror made her flounder and desperately struggle in Vayne's arms.

"Light!" she cried, and Vayne immediately echoed her demand. The room burst into illumination. Vayne blinked against it and frowned into her face.

"What's wrong?"

Putting as much distance between them as possible, a ludicrous effort, seeing as her body was fully aware of his proximity and its own potential, Neira called upon her military training to school her brain. She couldn't become Vicky and lose herself. "Who did I give you? Did you recognize the names?"

Vayne didn't appreciably relax his hold, but he backed off his intensity and she shored up her withered defenses. Working with him out of necessity had wreaked havoc on her determination to reject his intention to bond with her. Trust him, indeed, on this one thing. It was like nibbling on a piece of dark chocolate when the entire box sat temptingly within reach. Bad, bad libido.

With a sigh, he searched her features, lifting one shoulder as he seemed to recognize her determination not to allow him any liberties. "I recognized several names you spoke, Neira. A few I've already taken action against. But it is difficult to judge whether the rest were shared within the context of the rout of the Juxtant, or otherwise, and I require evidence. Baraith would have received updates of the last stands, hence the use of those names, perhaps, but there is a chance he would also have been continuing to forge and sustain alliances. He was always one to plan ahead, and he would never plan to surrender. So it would stand to reason he'd remain in contact with those he was engaged in for other nefarious purposes.

"The descriptions will be catalogued and compared for evidentiary purposes. It won't take long. And then we shall see. I have reached out to my hunters of both Baraith and those who perpetrated the unconscionable act on our species, so your additional pieces of that puzzle will be of help."

The side of Vayne she'd barely glimpsed before— the one also written about during the earlier war—was suddenly apparent. If she squinted she'd see the similarities to the Juxtant cousins he disparaged and disdained, and she knew there would be no mercy afforded to either her tormentor or those cowards who'd used genetic warfare, pinpointing the Shadalla women and children. That lack of mercy didn't bother her at all.

He slipped out of the bunk and she willed her eyes to look elsewhere, anyplace but at his fine ass and broad, muscled back. Had he really been intent on stealing her control? Or merely sharing her burdens? Neira was back to feeling conflicted and very concerned Vayne was wearing her down. And she felt abandoned yet desperate to make sense of things.

After entering something on the data display, he touched a corner with his thumb. "There. It's done."

"It seems strange that of all women, all Home World women, you would come across me." It was like she had no will of her own. Rather than avoid any conversation about fate as she'd planned, she had to go put it right out there. Damn it. It certainly didn't help that they were both nude. "And that I miraculously would be one of your chosen and perhaps possess the means for you to obtain your ultimate revenge."

Vayne stilled in the same way he'd done when she'd last spoken her mind. It was a tell of sorts, and she filed it away. He then smiled, such a wide, genuine smile she nearly smiled back. But she didn't, because just as quickly his expression took on a resigned cast. She wanted to look away, away from what was surely hurt, and his naked body should have been the distraction, but she couldn't do it. This couldn't be resolved by lust.

"What?" she demanded instead.

"Do you think this is a conspiracy, then? Something cleverly constructed with the timing so exact and all the players fulfilling their tasks so perfectly? I suppose it could happen. I have already established my belief in fate. But a conspiracy must feel more likely to you than trusting in the idea we are destined for one another, and we crossed paths to complete the circle. And that you have developed feelings for me as I have for you. I ascribe to the latter."

"I'm not the only one for you," she said stubbornly. "You might have waylaid another transport, raided an outpost and spied your chosen."

A curious look flitted over his face and she tried to interpret it, for it seemed important that she do so. Was that fear she saw? Impossible. His next comment was going to have a terrible impact. She could feel it.

"I've indeed botched this, haven't I? Right from the beginning. And your conspiracy theory has only strengthened your resolve while I believe in what was meant to be. That we were destined." He paced away from her and ran a hand through his hair, showing her a certain discomfiture that was sadly disturbing. "I thought to use the influence of the Shadalla pheromones to seduce you, make you mine and elicit your surrender. Because I am impossibly drawn to you and I do not lie about how my feelings have developed into…more. And despite how effectively you resist, there is something between us, quite separate from my…advantage. But it can never be simple, at least not for me."

The laugh he then gave was self-deprecating. Neira made enough of those sounds in her life to know, and she peered at him, puzzled. She found she didn't want to ask, but the words slipped past her lips anyhow. "I don't follow."

"There is a holding period, a grace period, if you will. It allows our chosen to acclimatize and settle within the male's sphere, aided by the pheromones, and give consent. I failed to mention that part, for fear you would withhold consent. I sensed that about you, and it follows, because you aren't Shadalla and haven't been raised since childhood to understand what that entails. You are the only chosen, in my experience, who has the wherewithal to resist. And I believe I now understand." He squared his shoulders and she followed the play of muscle across his torso, aware she might not wish to hear what he had to say next.

"I cannot have it both ways. Destiny—fate—has seen fit to put you in my path, and because of this I will soon have the last of those responsible for the planned extinction of my people. But fate is also cruel, and I am obviously not meant to have you as my lifemate. Perhaps because by being the sovereign sacrifices must always be made. Revenge has become an empty alternative but it appears it is all I will have." Vayne finished shrugging into his tunic, having stepped into his leggings, and he moved to the door. "Rest, Neira. I will return when I have news."

She snapped her mouth shut, aware she'd been staring after him in shock, and warred with such a sense of loss as to hollow out her insides. His parting speech should have reeked of self-pity, like a child denied a coveted toy. But instead, it was spoken quite matter-of-factly, the pain it hid barely leaking through. But she felt it deeply and wished for him to return so she could soothe him. Her body missed him equally.

No amount of rearranging the bedclothes, none of her efforts to swaddle herself like a small child, was enough to ward off the head-to-toe chill that swept over her. She needed Vayne for that, as she knew he needed her. She'd suffered the ague as a young teen and thought she might die from it, regardless of the medicines available then, even to the poor, and this hurt far worse. The body might not recall pain despite the mind's ability to remind one of the experience and warn against it, but Neira had no difficulty in contrasting the two. She shivered and shook and suffered against the ache in silence, the only thing she could master against it. If the pheromones he spoke of weren't having the anticipated impact on her, what was? A four letter word spelled out across her whirling thoughts and she automatically erased it. But the faded outline remained.

****

Vayne made his way to the bridge, pretending he wasn't running from Neira and refusing to think about anything other than completing the task at hand. He'd spoken from his hearts, handed them to her without thought, and he'd never been so discomfited. But there was the matter of getting home safe, so he needed to focus, though he suspected that if he cut the serpent's head off, its tail would shortly determine the lack of direction and fly back home.

"Sir." Leric was back at his post. His exec appeared weary—and extremely happy. The bridge crew looked pained and kept their distance. Vayne, too, felt the lack and it was like a whisper of the lash across his senses. He envied the other man fiercely and took a breath to let it go.

"Anything from our hunters?"

"Not yet. But soon. How is your chosen? That information she recalled was priceless." Leric didn't inquire how Neira came to have that data, and Vayne wasn't about to share. The other man knew about the medical emergency of earlier and was a master at putting things together but would never voice his findings unless he believed them to be necessary. It was what made him the best man for the job and an officer Vayne could not imagine doing without.

"She's fine. And the word from Nibiru?"

A quick blink was the only indication Leric had noted Vayne's brusque reply. "Jurlek advises the message has been sent. We will wait at the rendezvous point. A good choice, by the way."

Leric had a way of stating the facts without fanfare or being obsequious and there was no man he'd rather have by his side when it came to traveling through space, either. He opened his wound. "How is your bride, Leric?"

His exec visibly swelled. "She is well. All is well. I had no idea of the wonder of bonding, Sovereign. I feel so fortunate."

"And Eltrast? Jurlek? What of them?"

"I believe they are progressing in the courtship. Somewhat slower." Leric's tone was tinged with pride at being first, and Vayne nearly smiled despite a pang in his chest.

"And what if the women had been aware of our…extra persuasion, Leric? Might the courtships have gone so smoothly?" He was aware he was challenging a dictate he'd put in place, and rubbing salt into that very raw personal wound, but it was both a ruler's prerogative and duty in regard to the former. As for the latter, perhaps he longed for the role of martyr. He pushed the thought aside. Pitiful.

Leric opened his mouth and shut it, his forehead creasing, and he looked away from Vayne, veiling his features. When he again faced him, his face was guileless. Perhaps Vayne had imagined that his exec was deliberately hiding something from him. "I believe others knowing how the Shadalla pursue our chosen would deem it overly tenacious and perhaps perceive it as stacking the deck to our advantage, but we would convince our brides regardless. And time has been of the essence, sir." His exec used another Earth euphemism. "Desperate times require desperate measures."

That simple, if vague, assessment should have reassured Vayne but he pressured Leric harder. "And if your Victoria learns you seduced her and she was, essentially, powerless to resist?"

Leric shook his head. Emphatically. "She is my chosen. And my only. She might complete me, but I have committed my hearts. And I owe her more than I can say. Lifemate holds true for all except those who were bonded through genetic manipulation." The other man paled and flinched. "I apologize, Sovereign. I am deeply sorry. I was thoughtless. Please blame it on my recent bonding."

"No, Leric. You were being honest and it's been a long time since Asula faded. I take no offense."

His exec clearly wished to speak further but maintained his silence, likely fearing another misstep. Vayne cursed himself under his breath. He'd been given an unheard of second chance and in his arrogance had failed to consider the variables. All Earth women were different and his chosen was possibly the most complex female he'd ever had occasion to meet. It was him who was lacking and now courted failure. How he wished she had turned to him, and not away.

"Sir?"

"What is it, Leric?"

His exec appeared to choose his words carefully. "Perhaps consideration can be given to finding other chosen in different ways once your quest is satisfied and the Juxtant are finished. I could envision contingents visiting the Home World and its colonies once our security is beyond reproach. Humans visiting our planet. That would provide opportunities and we would perhaps not need to hide our lack of procreative options. Because we both know how compatible our species are. Humans could appreciate what we have to offer. We need not speak of our desperation, but suggest a joining of our species in the interest of maintaining peace."

"Well spoken, Leric. Something to ponder once

we have matters in hand." And if he'd failed with his chosen, others could learn from his loss. The weight of such a thing caused him to seek out his chair, where he brooded, watching and waiting for word. His exec retreated to his own station, respecting his sovereign's obvious request for space.

The crew moved quickly and efficiently about their tasks and prudently ignored him. No doubt they'd chewed over his confession to Neira and while, generally speaking, the word of the sovereign was law and willingly adopted as thought and action by his people, they had to know something hadn't gone according to plan given his presence here. When he should be bonding with his chosen.

"Sir." Leric broke into Vayne's train of thought and he focused on his exec, who was tapping away on his display. "Ambassador Rush's name has come up three times. I've confirmed it with all sources."

The lassitude that plagued him since his revelation about Neira and his own ineptness was replaced with a sense of elation. So his intuition had been correct, back when he'd seduced Rush's daughter, Fiona. The man's reaction to him had teased the senses, a mixture of fear, scorn and cunning. The fear had obviously won out, unless someone with more brains had warned the ambassador. Vayne had no idea who had assembled the assassination teams, but Rush used Fiona as the reason to expel Vayne and bar him from Earth after he'd escaped. Now it appeared the man was a still-living culprit, linked to the unleashing of the genetic weapon.

"Who does he have ties with?"

Leric consulted his display. "No one alive from that time except for Senator Annis. They have considerable history. Matriculated together and ran in the same circles. Same political leanings. Annis is presently in an advanced care facility. Old age complicated by Winns disease. Your chosen shared his name as well."

Winns was easily contracted by humans who traveled to certain planets, Ureses being one of them. The unfortunate Mr. Winns had been the first to die from the disease, for which there was still no known cure. "Map his itinerary for the past decades, at least two before the war. Compare against what we know about Baraith's." Humans lived well over a century with proper medical care and nutrition, and Annis would have had the best of those options, so his culpability was entirely probable.

He waited patiently, and within a few moments Leric confirmed the old man's travel to Ureses and another of those planets. There was no apparent good reason for him to have been on either. The timing provided him the opportunity and access to Baraith on both, sealing his fate. "Have him removed from the facility and dumped in one of the ghettos."

"It's likely he'd succumb to Winns within the year, Sovereign." Leric offered another option as dictated by his status. "Or he could be terminated at once."

"Or he can live out that year without comfort, alone and without resources. Wandering aimlessly." Neither he nor Leric were under any illusions as to what twelve months with that disease in the slums would be like for Annis. It wasn't enough suffering after what he'd done. Those in the ghettos tended to torture and taunt the crazy ones, rather than kill them, so the old man might pay the entire time. The hunters would carry out his orders and no doubt be happy to return home with a hostage.

"Yes, sir. And the ambassador?"

"Have him brought here. Recall all the hunters from Earth."

"Not take him to Nibiru, then?" His exec knew

that execution needed to happen publicly for Rush, once he'd confessed his crimes, but that was a moot point. He would confess and the Shadalla would have at least one mentally competent individual to see punished—but Vayne required the man on the *Tomodr* far more at the moment.

"We have a blockade to breach, Leric. Bring the ambassador here. He has a variety of uses." *And I have the need to face him personally before he is held on Nibiru.*

"Sir."

That left Baraith, and perhaps Rush would prove helpful in that regard as well. Vayne waited for the serenity that should rise and soothe him, knowing he'd found the last of those responsible—and still alive—for the genetic crime. But while he could admit to a certain satisfaction, he couldn't settle.

"I'll be in my quarters. Alert me to any changes and to the arrival of our ships. And of the ambassador." He'd lay odds Rush would arrive first, the hunters' small predator craft being quick and difficult to track.

Leric acknowledged him, and Vayne pushed to his feet, suddenly weary and in need of his lifemate. Her proximity would nurture him and the irony wasn't lost. He should be meeting *her* every need, rather than expect her to assuage his.

Once again entering his cabin, Vayne was struck by Neira's natural, spicy scent as it surrounded him, a fragrance forever etched on his senses. He inhaled deeply and approached the bunk, wondering who was the master and who, the captive. He laid a hand on her shrouded form and she came up off the mattress in a welter of flailing limbs, right into his arms. She was shivering, her lips nearly blue with cold and Vayne cursed himself for leaving her.

Cuddling her close, he murmured, "I have you, little warrior. I have you."

In time she was soothed and he marked the moment when her demeanor changed from that of a lost waif both seeking and offering solace to…something vastly different. Something passionate and wanton. All his angst and soul searching fell away as his dominance surged to replace it, Neira's telegraphed need so dire he had no choice but to meet it.

He managed to lay her shaking body upon the bunk, reluctant to put any space between them but desperate to remove his clothing—the better to experience the heated velvet and silk of her against his naked flesh.

"Hurry." Neira's moan spurred him on and his tunic joined his leggings in less than a stint.

Her face was flushed with desire and this time her golden eyes were dilated with lust and not fear. As he watched, the tip of her tongue crept out to moisten her short upper lip. Vayne tried to rein in his beast but lost all semblance of control when she reached between them and stroked his pulsing cock. She wasn't hard to pin beneath his weight, soft in all the right places even as her toned body fit against his with no give. He wrestled her hands above her head and fastened them into the cuffs with the ease of long practice.

"No." Her breathing changed from passionate soughing to restricted pants.

"It is our way, little warrior. Especially this first time." He remembered his promise to explain about the restraints and how he'd been distracted. "Neira. I won't hurt you. You have my word."

Thick, black lashes cloaked her gaze, blocking his read on her and his hearts hammered with fear that she would refuse him. "I can't be restrained."

"You can. With me." Vayne stared into her eyes as her lids fluttered open and let her see into him. "If you touch me this first time, even in passion, a…part of me…will construe it as interference, resistance, and I'll get rough with you. I won't allow it."

Inch by infinitesimal inch her glorious body relaxed beneath him as she gave him her trust, and Vayne had never felt so honored. He wanted to ask about her change of heart. Why she'd responded to him and needed him so badly that her arousal perfumed the room and she fairly seethed with yearning, but he ascribed to one of the Home World's sayings. Never look a gift horse in the mouth. Although how a nearly extinct quadruped might compare to his lifemate was beyond him, except for the wild, untamed part of her. And the beauty. And the fact she was also one of a kind.

Leaning in, he kissed her, absorbing the taste and feel of those firm lips, pressing firmly and possessively before licking along the seam in a quest for the treasure within. On a whisper of a moan Neira parted for him and he slipped inside the moist cavern, working over her teeth, testing her palate before teasing her tongue with his own. Only when he knew she required more air than what she'd drawn through her flaring nostrils did he pull back, and her tawny eyes blinked open.

"You taste like *mel*, sweet and smooth and golden."

"Honey?"

"The same." Vayne set his lips against her temple, pressing kisses downward, over the curve of her cheek, the sharp angle of her jaw and the long length of her neck. He paused to nibble at the pulse that beat so quickly there, his hearts speeding up in response. Tearing his mouth away, lest her response pull him too quickly, he shifted to place a knee on either side of her waist and sat back. This was something he refused to rush, no matter how his beast insisted he take her immediately. "Lights."

Neira flinched and blushed. An actual pink flood of color washed over her cheeks.

Knowing he loomed over her, something that gave him great satisfaction, he checked her for fear and was relieved to see nothing but embarrassment. Placing a finger just below the hollow of her throat, he traced a light path along her body to the top of her pubis. "Beautiful."

Neira squirmed and tried to look away but he pinned her with his gaze. "I've seen you naked for days, little warrior. Washed every inch of your body. Why are you shy?"

Visibly searching for words, whether the ones she thought he wanted to hear or the truth, she finally answered him. "This is intimate. I don't do sex this way."

He'd been correct not to put her beneath him and thrust into her wetness, then, despite the nonverbal consent. Still, he wasn't going to ask for it now. If she refused him, then she did, but he wasn't asking. His beast nodded its approval via his cock and he used his other hand to stroke it. Neira's gaze locked on the movement and her red nipples pebbled harder. "This isn't merely sex, Neira. Understand that."

Vayne held his breath. Of course he had to gain her consent, his beast be damned. His moral compass served him well in this regard, at least. Neira bit the corner of her bottom lip, something so curiously erotic yet out of character that he immediately wanted to kiss her again.

"I need you, Vayne. I suffered while you were gone. I tried to hate you for making me dependent in any way, however you did it. But dammit, I need you to fuck me."

"Do you consent?"

"I'm in your cuffs and not screaming the place down, and I'm not trying to kick your balls into your throat. I'd say that's consent."

"Neira." His *balls* rested on the patch of hair decorating her mound, a delightful, soft, whiskery nest, and he had only to shift his body a few *parsis* to fit his anxious cock against her opening. Plunge deep inside of what had to be heaven. He could feel the heat radiating up from the apex of her thighs, calling to him, and her scent made him mad. He chose his response deliberately. "I can fuck any number of females—"

She tensed and glared, that mouth he'd just plundered and caused to swell like a blossom now flattening into a thin line.

"—but you are not merely any female. You are my chosen."

"I can't, Vayne. I can't be your chosen, not forever. But I need you." Despite his own frustration and anguish he nearly laughed at the miserable look on her face.

"What is it you truly fear?" he asked carefully.

"Losing myself. If I am to live, then it has to be on my terms and not as a mere extension of Vayne Palldyn."

With a heavy heart he swung off of her and to the floor, reaching for his uniform leggings. It nearly killed him to withdraw from her and his beast snarled impotently. Neira let out a sound suspiciously like a sob behind him and he turned to see her tug herself back with the cuffs to sit up against the head of the bunk. She watched him with a guarded expression and curled her legs under her as he once again freed her wrists. He resolutely didn't look at her breasts and found it painful to even match her stare. What was there to say? "I have news."

She blinked and swallowed hard, visibly shifting to follow his new line of thought. "Did you find him?"

"Not Baraith. Yet. But the last two living conspirators are mine. And it's you I have to thank." He moved to release her hands and she grabbed at the linens to pull them over her, obviously cold again. Vayne called for more heat in the cabin and paced to the chair.

"Will you tell me the plan?" Her flushed cheeks belied the calm question, and her arousal wafted to his nostrils.

"Of course." Somehow he gained control. He shifted to ease the aching of his balls and shaft, concentrating on the fact his little warrior would know he'd have a plan. She was his perfect counterpart and how could she not understand that? Quickly sharing what he'd doomed Annis to, he marked a brief flare of distaste on her lovely face before she nodded.

He took a deep breath, a mistake, because she smelled so damn good. "And the ambassador will be here as quickly as my hunters can arrange it."

"You'll have the military after you in full force."

"No. I have complete confidence that Rush will be taken without a trace, no evidence left, and his absence will be explained only if I wish it."

"You'll use him as barter to get past the Outriders? To ensure we get to Nibiru safely?" Neira rested her hand against her throat and he admired the long lines of it. Was he wrong to experience a frisson of hope when she spoke of his planet as her destination?

"I will use him if necessary."

Huddling beneath the blanket, Neira again chewed on her lip. "You would let the entire, sordid mess come to light? Won't that give the Home World unwanted insight? They'll learn about your need for females to continue your species. You'll be giving up a tactical advantage."

Ah, his little warrior, ever the soldier. Not daring to touch her, his beast roiling beneath the surface of his control and raving to join with her, Vayne contented himself with a shrug. "As you pointed out earlier, it was but a matter of time."

She stared at him, then slowly shook her head, never taking her gaze from his. "You're doing this for me. Because of me."

"You are my chosen. I'll protect and defend you to the death."

A huge tear gathered in the corner of one eye before escaping the confines of her lashes and rolling down her cheek. Vayne could have sworn he heard it splash down, given his heightened senses and how in tune he was with her. He somehow stayed sitting, very nearly past the last of his famed self-control. He might have gone to her, whether to comfort or take her as his own he didn't know, when the display signaled a request to enter.

Neira broke her stare and faced away from him toward the hull. Vayne shoved to his feet, grateful for the interruption because he could see no way to breach the impasse. Time was running out on all fronts. He keyed the door open and the panel slid wide to display his medic, Stenlor. The other male's eyes were wide with apprehension and Vayne frowned.

"What is it?"

"Sovereign, I signaled you via the com but there was no response. And I believe you must see this."

Vayne cast a look at the display panel. He'd forgotten that it had been set for bridge traffic only, considering their current state of readiness. He reached for the tablet clutched in Stenlor's hand. Scanning the information, he raised his eyes to the other male's, and the medic gave a confirming nod.

"How? Do you have an explanation?"

"No. I've set more tests to run while I came here, sir. We aren't as well equipped for this kind of research on the *Tomodr* but I entered everything I had and what seemed applicable from the data banks."

Vayne stepped out into the corridor, using his bulk to force the medic along the hall. "You're aware that my chosen is resisting me."

Bowing his head, Stenlor grunted an acknowledgment. The little scene in the ship's mess had indeed been bandied about. But Vayne didn't care. There was something momentous here and while he had yet to process it completely, it didn't feel horrible. A thought struck that burgeoning sense of hope dead. He waited until he could be certain of sounding as befitted a sovereign and not a man hopelessly enamored by a feisty *leicat* of a woman.

"Would…involvement with another of our kind, even someone less evolved, have caused this ability?" The other male didn't know what had caused Neira to break down, only that she had and required medical support. He'd done the compatibility testing at the same time, something else Vayne was certain he was going to suffer for when Neira found out. But in the meantime the thought of Baraith… A knife to his gut would be more palatable.

Immediately, the medic shook his head. "Nothing in our files would support that theory. I thought of it, of course, considering our species' inclination to dabble with otherworld females. But there would be evidence in her genetic markers and there is none. Your chosen has never been bonded and nor has she borne children."

"But if she has the ability to resist—it's not me? I am producing—"

"Yes, sir. In goodly amounts. It was apparent when I determined the likelihood of procreation. Your pheromones are more prevalent and potent than Leric's, which is why it is so puzzling. You and the Earth human are a near-perfect match and offspring are a certainty."

Only if he was successful in getting his seed inside of her, Vayne thought ruefully, keeping his features impassive. "Near perfect?"

"Well, she isn't Shadalla."

"Thank you, Stenlor. Keep this confidential and encrypt all files. We may soon be face-to-face with representatives of the Home World and I haven't yet decided what they should be privy to. And, when possible, I want you to seek information on all the other otherworld females and their Shadalla mates. I will personally consult with Leric."

The other man's head tilted and he got a faraway look on his face. The medic wasn't only an excellent physician but a brilliant scientist too, one who loved space travel. Vayne was suddenly beyond pleased Stenlor was along on this trip.

Focusing again, Stenlor nodded. "I take your point, Sovereign. This puts a very different face on things. One that excites the scientist in me. It couldn't be something terribly obvious and very unlikely any of the males would overtly share because of bringing their bond under scrutiny."

"Then get on it. We have but a short period of time."

"Of course." Stenlor took the tablet back and hustled away. Vayne stared after him and weighed his approach with Neira. But first he needed to speak with his executive officer. The sovereign never went into war without every scrap of intelligence he could gather, and this was a battle he intended to win.

"Vayne?" He whirled to see Neira, wrapped in bed linens, standing in the doorway. He hadn't heard her move, hadn't detected her and surely that was a good portent—he had no requirement to protect himself against her any longer. With the exception of his hearts and soul, and it was far too late for that.

He moved toward her and she shuffled into their quarters. "Sovereign's duty again, my little warrior. I'll be back as soon as I am able." He risked dropping a kiss on her forehead, mightily pleased when she didn't flinch away and even leaned into him.

Stepping back before he gathered her up and took her back to bed to show her what he'd just learned, and what he hoped to confirm, he exited the cabin, the door sighing shut in her surprised face.

Chapter Eight

Neira frowned, feeling her eyes squint and her jaw drop when Vayne vanished from sight. The damned alien kept doing that. Her emotions were a jumbled, hot mess in direct contrast to how chilled she was yet again. Damn the man and his lofty ideals. While she'd accepted it wouldn't be a quick tumble with him, she'd actually hoped he'd compromise his long-range plan and lay with her, maybe a few times. Now where the hell had that quaint term come from? She was no blushing maiden from those ancient tales and he was most certainly not a knight of old. No, only a *sovereign.* She stomped to the cleansing room, allowing her makeshift robe to drop to the floor before she entered the shower stall. It was easier to feel frustrated and unsatisfied than to dwell on that statement he'd made. The one that both made her heart swell and broke it at the same time. *You are my chosen. I'll protect and defend you to the death.*

Wrenching on the knobs, she stood under the fine, heated spray and reached for the soap. As she washed the signs of her arousal away, she brooded. Damn freaking pheromones. He had such an unfair advantage. Not to mention the far more important peace of mind he'd somehow imparted. But she couldn't give herself to him fully. It went against everything she was, now that her soul was healed. By him. *Argh.*

Punching the unforgiving wall of the shower didn't do anything other than make her knuckles swell and she surveyed them glumly, flexing her fingers and noting the faint marks around her wrist. She froze and cautiously turned her head, reaching to turn off the cleansing unit, listening hard. Nothing. But Vayne moved silently, so he could be out there. Or someone else could.

She chose a towel and wrapped the fabric around her, the moisture in her short hair dripping onto her shoulders as she crept to the doorway and surveyed the cabin. Empty. Her breath soughed out of her with an audible *whoosh* and she smiled faintly at her paranoia. He hadn't secured her before leaving and what might that mean? Crossing to the chest where he stored the clothing, she lifted the lid and spied the clothing she'd donned on the *Astris* that day of being boarded by the pirates. Even her briefs were there, and she grabbed her outfit and pulled it on. The leggings were slightly tight across her ass and she scowled. All that food of late by his hand and limited exercise had caused her to gain weight despite the angst she'd experienced—or maybe because of it—and her joints wouldn't tolerate the extra pounds. A soldier took care of her body or paid the price in the field. *You aren't in the field, Neira.* Right, and now she was talking to herself, if not out loud. She'd never been troubled by this kind of soul searching before and no doubt that was Vayne's influence as well. She might not be a soldier ever again, but there was always a call for mercenaries and defenders.

The polished mirror reflected a tall, straight and slender form with spiky black hair. Her skin had a quality it hadn't shown for some time, clear and glowing. She was the picture of health, and her eyes regarded her solemnly. Neira placed her hand against the cool surface and nodded to the woman in the mirror who reached back, pretending there wasn't a crippling ache in the middle of her chest. She could, and would, do this. She'd convinced the sovereign of her refusal to become part of him, to complete him and lose herself. It had been apparent in the resignation written across his handsome face and simmering in his amazing eyes. Even the proud stance had been affected, and while it bothered her, she'd do what was right. He'd find another chosen once this nonsense with the Outriders was dealt with and all of the Home World made aware of the perfidy of those monsters.

Humans no longer tolerated such heinous crimes, at least in the short term. History would no doubt fade and greed and need would prevail again, but there would be any number of women willing to immigrate to Nibiru if that planet opened its borders. Neira, although she had no talent for public speaking outside of rallying her troops, would lend her voice to it. She'd help turn what could be regarded as a vulnerability into an opportunity. And if the idea tasted sour to her, it wouldn't to others. Vayne deserved the opportunity too.

She examined the display panel closely, having made the bunk, tidied the cabin and the cleansing area and explored the contents of the chest and the various drawers situated around the cabin. Locating her *palka* and dagger had felt like meeting old friends, but she left them tucked away. And she tried not to think about some of the things she'd found. Shadalla sex toys, similar to the ones she'd seen on the Home World, in different colors and materials, filled two drawers. She'd forced herself to run a finger over them, feeling them as inanimate objects, crushing the fantasies they created, and slowly her libido had returned to normal. This was just another reason for her to stand firm against him. He made her crazy with lust by merely looking at her and being so unconcernedly naked in her presence. If he were to use other things to wreak his sexual magic, there was no telling what he would expect from his chosen when that woman *completed* him, for how could a mindless sex slave give informed consent? Her decision bolstered, Neira had shut the drawer and put it out of her mind.

The display screen could open up a wealth of

possibilities if only she could access it but of course it required a designated thumb or palm print. The sovereign had recently programmed it to allow her to control the lighting and apparently the heat levels, so it was pleasantly toasty now. She really needed total access. But even if she could overcome Vayne how would she get his hand up this high? She laughed out loud. Getting the drop on him was no longer part of her agenda—*trapped, in space, remember?* But she itched to contribute to the upcoming confrontation, contribute her military skills now that the issue of lifemates and bonding was off the table, and wished he'd come back so they could have a discussion. She absolutely wasn't wondering how he might employ that curiously shaped…what the fuck was wrong with her?

The door sighed open and the subject of her thoughts sauntered in, causing her heart to pound. Unbidden, her eyes ate him up from the top of his thick hair to the sizable feet, and she convinced herself she hadn't lingered on any parts in between. Vayne paused and scrutinized her in the same manner and with a great effort Neira kept her feet glued to the floor. Her leggings were soaked despite her briefs and it was all his fault.

"I leave you untethered and to your own devices and you promptly disobey me," he observed, a wry note in his voice. "Clothed and prowling my quarters."

"Did you really expect me to be waiting, naked in your bed?" Good grief. Was she flirting with the man? Her tone hadn't been sarcastic or even challenging. Neira had no idea how to flirt. She'd been more of a get-down-and-dirty kind of girl because it had been more about satisfying a physical need than about romance. *Never* about romance. And neither was this. This was seduction by alien species and something she'd obviously had no control over. Thank goodness it had been put to bed. No pun intended.

"I'd hoped to find you there." She watched him advance the short distance to stop so close she could feel his warmth. Could he smell her desperate need?

"I was cold." Not entirely true, seeing as she'd called for that temperature increase. The shower had warmed her and wearing clothes helped. Not to mention her rabid fantasies.

Vayne obviously saw through her subterfuge, seeing as his quarters were plenty warm, but he played along. "I regret that. I keep the cabin cooler because we Shadalla aren't as sensitive to temperature, and I neglected to raise the heat when I left earlier. But I do prefer you naked."

She preferred him naked too but this giddiness had to stop. Where was her earlier resolve from not even an hour ago? Right out the proverbial window with her inability to contain her arousal. "I'd like to discuss what's going to unfold with the Outriders. I hope I can contribute."

The frown that marred his pleasant countenance told her he didn't want to entertain that idea, and he confirmed it. "You won't be any part of it."

"I can help," she argued, reaching for that part of her that gave her control.

"Neira. Little warrior." Wry humor and frustration warred in his tone. "I don't want the Home World to have further reason to harm you. I would prefer they not have a confirmation you are on the *Tomodr*."

"They might not have that in mind. Harming me." Sure. Like it wouldn't be the easiest answer. Wipe her out of existence and if it meant taking out a sovereign what did it matter to people who still controlled the military for their own ends? They might even see it as evening the odds. Except Vayne had Ambassador Rush, and Annis was no longer a threat, so her idea of exposing their actions and educating the people back home seemed obvious. She told him of her musings.

"I like the latter part," he agreed. "You can be most persuasive, and the idea of Home World women willingly offering to mate with Shadalla is ideal. But even if we can negotiate with the Home World, Baraith is still at large and you could be at risk."

"Why? It's not like I determine the outcome of what you intend for him." Unless she got to the biggest monster first by some twist of fate. That idea vastly appealed, because she wouldn't be a weak, unarmed victim, weighted down by her memories.

"You are my chosen and Baraith would take great enjoyment in dispatching you." Something terrible flashed in the depths of Vayne's eyes and she tried to interpret it.

"He'd do that? To deny you a longer life?"

She didn't see him move, yet she was pinned helplessly against the bulkhead, up on her toes and nearly unable to take a breath. "To destroy me, Neira," he grated, those turquoise eyes boring into her own, full of lust, heat and pain. "I might not fade, but life would hardly be worth living."

He kept pledging himself and she desperately wanted to acquiesce, so she thought instead of the contents of that drawer and how she wanted to hang on to her identity.

As if collecting himself and getting his emotions under control he set her on her feet and smoothed his hands down her arms, muttering an apology. He stepped back and an unconvincing smile curved his lips. "Might we talk about something else?"

"O…kay." Neira slipped past him and perched on the edge of the bunk, leaving him the option of the chair.

Déjà vu.

"I just spent time with Leric and Victoria. After Stenlor stopped by—the medic who treated you."

Right, the other guy who had witnessed her breakdown. She nodded, wondering what Victoria and Vayne's exec had to do with anything.

"Stenlor conducted some tests on your blood." At her stiffening, Vayne raised his hand in a request for silence, not unlike the ones her former superiors had made and Neira subsided. "He took a sample while administering medication when you experienced the dissociative fugue."

"I suppose being a captive precludes any refusal I might have made," she muttered, her arousal now a simmering memory. It was good to be reminded of her circumstances and how she came here, kind of like a cold bucket of water thrown in her face.

"I was certainly operating within that purview. Then."

She snapped her attention to him. Vayne sounded extremely apologetic and remorseful. "Excuse me?"

"I can't say I'm not pleased that he did so, even if my reasons were perhaps something you won't appreciate. I wanted to know if you could conceive, although I'd already decided I couldn't give you up."

"And can I?" She felt both bitter and curious, and decided to ignore the latter part of his statement for fear she'd curl up in a ball at his feet.

"We are a near-perfect match."

So there would be someone out there who'd *be* a perfect match. That helped to diminish her ridiculous urge to connect with him. Well, no bother. She'd made her decision, after all. Neira pressed her fist against her diaphragm but managed not to double over at the thought of him with that someone else.

"Neira?" Vayne knelt at her feet and peered up into her face. "What's wrong?"

"Nothing. Just a cramp or something." She took her hand away and leaned back, and Vayne, after a long look, returned to the chair.

"Not only are we a match, you are impervious to my bonding pheromones, or at least able to resist them," he continued.

That nugget of information dropped into the swirling morass of her thoughts and she fumbled for it, knowing its portent. Vayne waited, patient as a big cat but also wary.

"So my attraction to you isn't because of pheromones?"

"No. Not the bonding pheromones but we definitely have other...chemistry."

The pain in her chest loosened a trifle. "Why did you go and see Victoria? And Leric?"

"To test a theory with a limited sample. I also inquired of Eltrast and Jurlek." Vayne hesitated and she could see him choose his words. "I've asked Stenlor to consider other Shadalla-human pairings, but that kind of information is best obtained face-to-face. Our traditions run deep, and because of the dearth of females it stands to reason the males who were graced by a chosen might not be forthcoming without absolute, credible reassurances. That there would be no interference."

"You're talking like a politician." Her heart hitched up a beat, knowing there was something life-changing on its way.

"I am a politician, Neira. Part of the burden of being sovereign."

"Fine, but can you just tell me?" She wanted to pace away from him or stick her fingers in her ears nearly as much as she wanted to hear him out. Her throat was dry and she felt a fine dew of sweat break out at her temples.

"It is entirely possible that bonding between our species lack some of the nuances Shadalla matings have. While the brain reaction is definitely there and our males recognize their chosen, thus pursue and seduce them with considerable...verve, the length of the process varies with each woman. To be expected, perhaps, given that we are compatible but not of the same species, so no one remarked on it. But that could infer the terms of the completion is different. So I inquired of Leric."

The vision of a besotted Vicky—a languid bundle of need caught up in the executive officer's arms—slipped across Neira's mind.

Vayne passed one big hand over his face, the palm rasping against the stubble on his chin. "While he doesn't have anything other than the words and stories of others who found their Shadalla lifemates long ago, he confirmed that there is a definite *distinction* between him and Victoria." He laughed. "It took my position and our friendship to wrest that from him, incidentally. Your fellow passenger might not have completely lost herself to Leric, but he would do anything to keep her. Including defying me. Lying by omission, a definite crime."

"Victoria fell in love with Leric? Without the other implications and influence?" Neira couldn't keep the doubt from her voice.

"It would appear so. I suppose the sex had something to do with it, as well."

Her gaze flew to his. "You're teasing me. You wouldn't have sex with me without consent to...more."

Silence stretched out as he continued to watch her, and she tried to hold on to her equilibrium as the last of the barriers melted away. There was no need for him to answer. The attraction she did her best to deny, to attribute to those pheromones, flowered and consumed her once again and this time she made no effort to control it. Chemistry without those other implications. Her breathing changed, louder in the space, at least to her ears, and she catalogued the way her body responded without the iron control of her mind. It was definitely lust and desire but upon learning it wasn't purely the result of advanced genetics she could admit to it being more. Wanting more.

Taking a deep breath, she spoke. "You ask a great deal of me."

"No more than I am willing to give."

She believed him, and what was more, now trusted him. And she knew he saw it too.

"Come here, little warrior."

****

Rising with the innate grace of the *leicat*, Neira moved to stand before him. Vayne never took his eyes from hers as he reached out to place a hand at her waist, just above the curve of her hip, splaying his fingers across the swell of her buttock. His touch resonated through the both of them, despite the layer of material, manifesting as a faint shiver in Neira and as a subtle shock wave up his arm. He closed his eyes the better to savor it, so secure in the belief she wouldn't take action against him in his vulnerability. Their connection had deepened and would flourish, and the perfection of that belief soothed every part of his soul.

Blinking open, he pulled his hand away and leaned back. "Remove your clothing."

Without hesitation his chosen swept the tunic over her head to bare her swelling breasts, the red nipples already beading with anticipation and her passion. She shoved the pants down, tiny briefs pulled along with the heavier fabric, and she stepped out, kicking the bundle away. He could scent her renewed arousal, her cleft slick and plump, and a growl escaped him.

Unbidden, she sank to her knees and he spread his own to allow her access. Neira shuffled forward, fitting her body close and Vayne granted her unspoken wish, those tawny eyes telegraphing her intent. He was painfully ready and despite the disconcerting amount of information he'd been showered with, he wasn't stopping to consider anything else. His female was in need of him and he, of her.

One of her slender hands passed over the hard bulge of him and he willed her to hurry, but she almost lazily worked the panel of his uniform leggings open, intent on her task, and an eternity passed before his cock was freed. Vayne moaned at her touch, her fingers tracing the raised ridges in his flesh, drifting over the sensitive cockhead, and he gritted his teeth to control the urge to thrust into her hands.

"Beautiful," she murmured, rubbing her cheek against him.

"Suck me." As a command it fell short, and the sovereign wasn't used to begging—ever.

He peered down at her as she lowered her head over him, pursing her lips tightly against any advance and his cock took up the challenge without any direction from him. It pressed harder against the seam of Neira's mouth and was granted access in excruciatingly tiny increments, slipping inside on her saliva and the enticement of her tongue. Little, come-hither strokes drew him ever deeper, and as commanded she began to suck him down, surrounding him with sensation until he was lodged deep in her throat.

His beast surged and Vayne set his hands on Neira's head, a benediction, before taking charge of the delightful task. She didn't resist, her own hands resting on his thighs, fingers clenching as he directed her mouth. He could make out the fan of her lashes across her flushed cheeks and was granted with the sight of those ripe lips as he pulled her away, only to wrench her back to take him again and again. She used her tongue with abandon and soon his strokes faltered as his orgasm boiled forth, his seed stored up for days as he waited for her to consent. He erupted into her throat, massaging that slender column as she swallowed him down, and he regretted only the loss of an opportunity to give her a child. When he carefully withdrew, his member wet and only slightly softer, Neira stared up at him, her mouth swollen once again. She looked well used—and satisfied.

"You please me, Neira." He sounded as gratified as he felt and she smiled mysteriously in response. Females—all females—appeared to appreciate their power, and Neira was most definitely female.

Standing, he stripped away his uniform, watching her watch him as she scanned his body, her golden eyes shimmering with lust. She accepted his hand and he lifted her to her feet, his arousal building impossibly again but now well within his control. He swept her up and swiveled to place her on the bunk, reveling in the way she relaxed into him. Straddling her, he traced the same line he had dropped kisses on earlier, wanting to believe he could see his mark. "My chosen."

Neira shifted restlessly beneath him, and Vayne accepted there was still much to discuss, but for now he would enjoy this time with her. Palming her breasts, he lifted the tender weight, his thumbs rubbing her nipples into tighter points. His breath caught in his chest when she raised her hands above her head toward the cuffs.

Wordlessly, he accepted her offer and buckled her in, pressing a kiss on each wrist. "You've already ensured my control with your clever mouth, little warrior. But this way I can bring you the greatest pleasure while you are powerless to gainsay me."

Neira's eyes dilated and her lips parted. Vayne observed her carefully for signs of distress but detected only arousal.

Dropping a kiss on her mouth, he smiled wickedly when she tried to capture him with those sweet lips.

"As you had your way with me, so shall I with you."

"Certainly, Sovereign." The obviously faked acquiescence in her voice was supported by the demureness of her gaze and Vayne ground his teeth. The gods of Isord hadn't lied when they forecast the lure of a submissive woman with a fiery spirit. What they'd failed to point out was that earning such a one's trust might dictate the strongest connection. And the most enduring one.

Returning to her breasts, he again lifted them and lowered his head, teasing each tender bud with his teeth and tongue, relishing Neira's tiny gasps and the way she tried to lift into his caresses. "Patience," he murmured, and laved the undersides, swirling his tongue over the silken flesh.

When he finally suckled her, Neira arched into his body, her long legs stretching and flexing restlessly behind him as he switched from breast to breast, assessing her breathy whimpers and near-silent pleas. She would scream his name before he was done with her and his cock filled again at the thought.

Taking his time, he followed along the delicate cage of her ribs with his lips, traversing the plane of her belly as fingers replaced his mouth, tweaking her nipples with devilish intent. So responsive. Had anyone taken their time with her? Had she ever enjoyed a lengthy sexual congress? Intimacy. His *leicat* feared it and he would teach her to never fear anything with him. She would never have that kind of privacy if he was to give her the pleasure she so deserved.

Licking past the cup of her navel, he traced her hip bones, marveling at the narrow breadth of her pelvis, hoping his child would soon be sheltered there, and on impulse he turned his head and rested his cheek against her satin skin.

Neira's breathing slowed and grew steady and they shared the long moment before he took up his quest. "Open your legs to me, little warrior."

Her long thighs parted and he inhaled deeply of her feminine musk, his beast stirring restlessly. He coaxed her legs further apart, bending them and setting her feet flat to allow him total freedom. Kneeling between them, Vayne stroked the soft skin with reverence before continuing upward to where her arousal glistened. Such a small, tight pussy with pouting lips the color of the fruit Neira liked at their morning meal. He dipped his head for a taste—tart yet sweet. She audibly sucked in air and he raised his face to ensure she saw what was written there, embodying what he felt. She blinked and everything in her eyes told his future. Their future.

It took effort to break their stare. The muscles in her belly rippled as he looked down at her center again. Crimson petals edged with pink, shining with her juices, the knot of her pleasure beckoning. Vayne had often refused such a summons but understood he could never resist his chosen.

Settling at her apex, his wide shoulders preventing any effort to hide her from him, he slipped his hands beneath her buttocks to tilt her for his best sensual attack and lowered an openmouthed kiss, his tongue lapping along Neira's slit in its entirety. Those long legs slid over his shoulders in an effortless motion and she whimpered and entreated him. But he worked at his pace, learning her, tasting her and rejoicing in his chosen. He sipped at her fount and she gave him more, fighting his hold as she chased an orgasm.

"Please, Vayne. Please." The cuffs rattled as she strained against them.

Ah, not yet screaming, although such impassioned sobbing was close. He sucked the tiny cluster of nerves between his teeth, flicking it with his tongue, and his little warrior came on a cry that echoed in the small space. Relentlessly, he drove her up again, worrying her clitoris and stroking into her clenching opening. He pressed his thumb against her tight rosebud, slick with the cream of her efforts, and gained entry as she went over again. Neira actually lifted his bulk from the mattress with a shudder and arch of her strong body, her heels hammering wildly against his back. He'd forever cherish the sound she made, a combination of his name and a prayer, and relented, petting her as she came back to herself.

Easing her legs to the mattress, he worked his body upward to lay on his side, close to her damp form, and kissed away the tears of extremis. His cock jumped at the touch of her skin and he shifted to lessen the torture. When at last her eyes fluttered open he fell into her yet again. His chosen.

"Okay?"

"Mmmm."

Propping his head on his hand, he leaned on his elbow and coasted his free hand over her, stroking first one breast, then the other, passing down her belly to cup her mound. Neira tightened her thighs around him and he obeyed her unspoken edict, content to simply hold her, knowing she needed a few moments. His beast rumbled again, not fully sated and definitely lacking patience, demanding it be unleashed.

Extricating his hand, Vayne worked the cuffs free and Neira brought her arms down with a grateful glance. He rubbed at her shoulders, alternating to ensure she was comfortable.

"That was…something."

"Merely something?" he teased.

"I would have stopped you pushing me into that second release if my hands were free."

"And you wouldn't have learned you are capable of falling again and again."

"You're an arrogant, smug male, Sovereign." But her accusation held no heat and he smiled at her. Smiling had not been in his repertoire over the past decades and it felt like a new experience each and every time Neira drew one from him.

****

There was definitely a certain freedom in having no choice. Especially when the one taking the choice away wasn't a threat. Well, maybe an intoxicating sensual threat but Neira figured she could come to accept that fact—easily. She then stirred a little in discomfort at the thought, because there were lots of other ramifications here. This wasn't about fucking and she knew that when she'd given it up. Even though there hadn't been any actual fucking…

As if reading her mind, something that seemed a very real possibility, Vayne began to caress her again. Neira could have interfered, could have grasped his wrist and pushed it away. She could have, but instead pushed into his touch, her nipples once again beading and aching with need. His mouth was amazing, surrounded by stubble that embodied the essence of the man—the alien. They truly weren't so different. She dared a cautious touch of his pectoral, then traced the scar nearby, wanting to press a kiss against it.

"Stabbed by our mutual enemy, little warrior," Vayne contributed as he trickled his fingertips toward her mound. "Under my armor somehow and straight into the heart."

She stilled. "Baraith? This is his work? How did you survive?" Her words tumbled over one another.

"The Shadalla have two hearts and our spleen has separate functions. Our vision is exemplary as is our hearing. We are also stronger than your species overall."

That explained the curious echo in his chest. The cadence had been off. "And you're okay?"

He shrugged, the movement causing his finger to jerk against her clit in a most enticing fashion. "Never better."

"Anything else I should know?" There was probably an enormous amount of information she absolutely didn't know, but one thing at a time.

He slid a finger inside her, the residue of those two amazing orgasms facilitating entry, although she felt restricted because her pussy was so swollen from those two amazing orgasms. That digit in her ass had been a new experience and, while it had felt strange at the outset, had definitely increased her pleasure. His finger dallied in a mysterious place at the front of her sheath and a spring deep inside of her began to wind tighter. "Anything else—about our physiology?" he asked.

When she didn't reply immediately, intent on the coiling of that spring, he spoke again. "Shadalla males have bigger cocks."

Somehow, she came up with a quip. "Really? I hadn't noticed."

Truth be told, his cock had barely fit in her mouth, and while she'd given head before she still wondered how she had conquered her gag reflex with Vayne.

Except it had seemed effortless.

He responded to her offhand comment, rising to loom over her with a glint in those turquoise eyes and she wished he'd put his magical finger back inside. "On the Home World I believe you'd be called a brat. Or a tease."

Neira arched her brows and fluttered her lashes. Lord, she was flirting again, only this time it didn't feel so foreign. Vayne dropped his weight on her and slanted his mouth over hers. He tasted like…joy and life. And that four letter word she couldn't yet voice but felt in her heart. Neira pulled him closer and inhaled, wanting him again.

He pulled back and she panted, reaching out, but he shook his head. "Hands and knees, little warrior."

If he'd called her his chosen she might have balked. Being taken from behind would assert his dominance even more, but he'd already taken her places she hadn't expected. She rolled over to take a position on her knees, bracing her weight against them and on her hands.

A finger traced the length of her spine and Vayne's heat blanketed her as he kissed first one shoulder then the other, nibbling at the nape of her neck until she bowed her head. The scarring didn't seem to put him off despite how he'd responded that first night. Curious how she hadn't even thought about it since. *Because he accepts all of you.*

"Chest to the bunk, Neira, bend your elbows. Yes, like that," he rumbled, his voice sounding pleased as she obeyed, her epiphany lost with his command.

She shivered and he immediately laid a hand on her back, soothing her. "Tell me."

"Again, I'm not used to being so intimate, giving up control." Although her hands weren't tethered.

"What I ask of you and you are willing to give is

received with my ultimate gratitude, Neira, and cherished. I will never take it for granted."

Holy shit. She melted at his words and the depth of emotion in his voice. Vayne coaxed her ass higher, sliding a pillow beneath her hips, and urged her thighs apart. When he slid a hand between them to test her wetness she bit her lip against a moan, her cheek pressing harder against the bunk.

He alerted her to his intent, the hard length of his thighs pressing against the base of her buttocks. She felt the difference in the texture of their skin and the wash of his breath as he leaned over her. As he traced the fine web of scarring on her back, the usual sensations of numbness and prickling pain weren't at all obvious, and she wanted to purr beneath the gentle touch—and acceptance. He stroked the curve of her hip. "Do you consent?"

"I do," she somehow choked out.

"Remain still."

She wasn't going anywhere, crouched before him, one hand under her chest and the other finding a purchase amongst the rumpled bed linens. The wide head of his cock slipped along her wet slit to bump her clit and she tried to control her flinch at its sensitivity. Vayne passed his shaft back and forth, slipping and sliding along her moistening folds and she held back a plea for more. Her vulnerable position, coupled with his expert teasing, began to break her down to her most female side, the one she'd denied since childhood. No longer needing to take care of herself and everyone around her. Her sovereign would shoulder that burden when she offered it. Right now she had but to receive.

"So wet. Almost time." She had to strain her ears to hear him.

One big hand slipped around her neck to pin her securely and for an instant she felt a flicker of panic before he notched himself at her opening and worked inside. Parting and stretching her swollen tissues, he gave her no quarter, and she embraced the pleasure-pain, courting a sense of fulfillment she'd never experienced. Vaguely registering the nestling of his sac against her when at last he bottomed out, Neira submitted. There was no shame in this, no embarrassment or need to prove anything. Nothing but to receive.

The tightness of his new grasp on her hip signaled his intent and Vayne took her without a hint of mercy. It was all about him, and his pelvis slapped against her ass in a measured beat, hard shaft thrusting deep to almost pull out before he drove deep again. Over and over until she could hear the slickness of the friction, hear the wet, grasping sound of her channel around him as he expressed his lust and hunger. He took her and claimed her, and her body responded, that coiled and primed spring boiling from her depths. Her breath expelled in frantic pants and her vision clouded. Vayne shoved his hand beneath her to unerringly seek out her straining clit as he stiffened and bellowed above her. His cock swelled impossibly larger, and hot seed flooded her deep inside as he pinched her nub and propelled her into the abyss.

Surrender was the ultimate freedom and she welcomed it.

Chapter Nine

Perhaps he required the full use of both of his hearts, after all. Vayne brought his ratcheted pulse down in increments and struggled to take his weight from Neira's crouched form. He reluctantly released the grip on her nape as his cock slipped out of her sweetly clasping sheath on a slip of their cum.

"Neira? My love?" She didn't move and he carefully turned her on her side, first gently freeing the arm folded beneath her chest, then inveigling her legs straight. He awkwardly rubbed the long muscles in her thighs and reached to do the same for her calves, admiring the slender length of her tidy feet. Everything about her was perfection.

She moaned and hitched onto her back, and Vayne gave her room, cramming against the bulkhead. His bed on Nibiru was commodious and there would be none of this fighting for space, although he treasured the closeness too. And Neira would never escape his touch no matter the size of their sleeping accommodation.

He sought for words to describe his state of being. Bliss was perhaps the closest he could come, with utter satisfaction being second. His balls felt pleasantly empty and his chest full. He wouldn't think about how near he'd come to losing her. There would still be challenges ahead, and not only between them. He would need to convince the status quo on his planet that definite changes were in store if they were to procreate and save themselves from extinction. The beatific state he enjoyed—as would those lucky enough to find their chosen—would be convincing enough if lifemates were found for those who would challenge him and his rule. His mind was already sorting through the possibilities, the curse of his position and duty when he wanted to enjoy the postcoital gift of his chosen.

Tucking Neira close, he drifted a light throw over her, noting that she no longer felt cold to the touch. He was overheated and famished and in a moment would summon sustenance but couldn't bear to leave her side even for the time required to reach the display panel. When she murmured and inched closer he sighed. This was the stuff poems and sonnets were written about, and he basked for another moment. The medic had detected a residual taint of birth control hormones in Neira's blood but such a small quantity that it was almost negligible. Vayne assumed it had been administered prior to her capture by the Juxtant and it spoke to her state of mind that she hadn't renewed the injection upon her discharge. It was unlikely that sex had been something she'd have wanted. That was something else he wasn't thinking about—what Baraith had done to her sexually. It was enough that monster hadn't spawned with her.

If he'd put a child in her today, Vayne would be past thrilled, but he selfishly wanted to have Neira to himself for some time. Time he knew she would require as well. Easing her slumbering form toward the other side of the bunk, he worked his way to the bottom, stepping over the clothing on the floor as he made his way to the display. Keying in his request for food, he then sent a message to Leric, asking for an update. The time he and Neira needed together would have to take place at a later date and preferably somewhere on Nibiru where there would be no risk of immediate requirement for him. Even a sovereign was entitled to—what had Neira referenced? A honeymoon. His cock stirred and he ignored it, heading into the cleansing area.

Returning to his sleeping room, wearing a loose pair of underclothes, he forced his feet to carry him to the door, rather than climb back into the bunk with Neira. He was in no way replete, but she would require time to rebound, if not physically, emotionally. As if he timed it, a crew member stood framed in the opening, balancing a tray of food with one hand raised to request entry. Vayne took possession of the container and the man, Brena, if he remembered correctly, made an attempt at saluting him gravely, but his face broke into a wide, pleased smile. The sovereign supposed the bonding was written all over him and he smiled back, surprising them both.

"Sir. Blessings."

"Thank you."

Brena shuffled backward and inclined his head before striding away. The news would be all over the ship in moments, and combined with all the other revelations they'd been treated to on this voyage, Vayne suspected it would prove to be fodder for weeks to come. And the ramifications? Years.

"That smells wonderful. I appear to have worked up an appetite." Neira moved into a seated position on the edge of the bunk, a sheet wrapped around her. Vayne viewed her with smug satisfaction, soaking in how well ravished she appeared, before schooling his features. His chosen didn't approve of arrogance, although possessed a certain amount of that trait herself.

"I ordered your favorites."

"You pay close attention, Vayne. Part of your charm." Her smile was wide and bright, but he didn't miss the hint of wariness in her tawny eyes.

"There is much I don't know about you, Neira, but we have the rest of our lives to learn about one another."

The smile became tremulous and she turned her attention to the food, and he didn't challenge her. He set the tray down and prepared them both plates. He would continue to feed her and provide for her needs, not yet ready to relinquish the privilege.

"I surrendered to you, Sovereign. Don't think I'm not aware. But now that we aren't sexually involved in the moment I'm struggling with it."

Vayne offered her a morsel to eat while he formulated a response, appreciating how honest she was being with him. Tell her bluntly or sweeten it? He decided on the former. "Of course you're struggling. Consider all that you've experienced, your history and your training. It wouldn't make sense for you to find surrender an easy thing. You honored me with your trust and granted me control. As I told you, it's not something I take lightly. Allow me to continue to prove that to you, my little warrior, because there is no going back."

She accepted a piece of fruit, chewing slowly, regarding him speculatively. "No going back? You couldn't be wrong? I no longer have a choice?"

"None. I will not let you go. You're stuck with me." He knew that levity with humans made difficult conversations more palatable.

"You were wrong about certain aspects of the bonding process with humans." Neira looked so solemn, her golden eyes grave and her brow furrowed.

"And pleased about that. I truly am because I don't want you to be any different than you are. But we *are* bonded." He heard the inflexibility in his tone and by the way her eyes flickered, she did as well. "Until death parts us."

"A contingency we didn't discuss," she said drily. "Your first lifemate faded—I know that was a genetic thing. But what happens to the female if the male dies in a true bond?"

How had they come to this discussion? *Because your chosen is bright and not easily dissuaded.* "I don't intend to fade anytime soon, Neira. But to answer your question, Shadalla females fade when their mates do unless there are children. Something to do with having a reason to live. More research must be carried out to determine if such is the case with human females."

"Lord. You're more like us humans than you know, Vayne."

Choosing not to pursue that comment, vaguely offended because he wasn't certain he wanted to have anything in common with humans other than Neira, he ensured she'd had enough to eat before urging her to the cleansing room. "Do you require my help?"

She snorted, a delightfully feminine sound. "No. I doubt we'd actually cleanse, and I'm well aware you have other things that will require your attention."

Watching her saunter across the small space, the sheet discarded, Vayne knew she was right and dragged his stare away, lest he be too tempted and give in to that lure. He surreptitiously rearranged his cock before he struggled into yet another uniform. Neither of them was wearing a stitch on that honeymoon. As he fastened the last closure, Leric contacted him. The message was brief. The ambassador was aboard and waiting his attention. Vayne was equally brief, directing that the hunters board one of the other ships, given that they were larger and could offer quarters, and the human male be placed in the one holding cell the *Tomodr* boasted. He wasn't going to give Rush any hint of hope. The man was adept at the games of politics and wouldn't be offered any opportunities or a sense of comfort. There would be no escaping the consequences of his perfidy.

He moved to the cleansing room and sucked in his breath at the sight of Neira rubbing her hair dry with a towel, droplets of moisture scattered over her shoulders and the tops of her breasts. A sultry, sensuous smile graced her lips when she saw him staring, and she set the towel down.

When one narrow brow arched at him, he collected himself and spoke. "Ambassador Rush has joined us. I'm going to go and charge him with the crime he committed, give him something to think about until we get to Nibiru."

"May I attend you?"

He was reluctant, and it had nothing to do with her being his lifemate and female. Rush and his cronies were the reason for the Shadalla's frantic search for females to perpetuate their species, and Neira was his because of that search so the issue was clouded with different emotions. No, he hesitated because he didn't want her to be in the presence of another monster and risk any reminder of her time of imprisonment and torture.

"Vayne?"

He sighed. "You may. But if it becomes too much for you…"

Moving with speed and surety, she stepped close, close enough for him to scent her, and he put his arms around her, astonished when she snuggled close. He'd expected to have to work harder for her affection outside of their bed.

"I'll be fine. I need to do this. It won't mean the same closure for me as for you, but as close as I'm going to get, unless you find Baraith and can take him alive."

He hadn't thought about it that way. If Rush had his way Neira would no doubt have been disposed of back in the hospital, without her connections and contacts. And most certainly would have met her demise on that mining planet. No loose ends. He nodded.

"I'll get dressed."

"Wear the *paca*."

There was only a slight hesitation before she

inclined her head against his chest, and he carefully set her away from him to retrieve the garment. Neira came to him naked, her skin glowing from being cleansed—and perhaps from his claiming—and stood quietly as he helped her into a pair of underwear. The feel of her beneath his hands shook his resolve, made him want to put off seeing Rush. As if she divined his thoughts she ran her fingers over his shoulders as he crouched before her, then brushed at his hair. He rested his forehead against her, dragging in her spicy scent and palming her buttocks.

"We should go," she murmured.

Ah, but he didn't want to leave these quarters, the scene of their ultimate commitment to one another, when a contemptible coward lurked a deck below and the journey home was fraught with danger. Vayne drew on his sovereign persona and stood.

Meeting her stare with his own, they didn't need to speak. Perhaps the bonding was different with humans but already he could practically read her thoughts—and she, his. His bride understood duty. He eased the *paca* over Neira's head. It drifted and settled about her as before but it seemed she wore it with even more regal grace.

Offering his arm, he waited until she set her hand on it and they exited his quarters—as a bonded pair. What should have been the proudest moment of his life was a trifle marred by what awaited him. Vayne grimaced ruefully. His thirst for vengeance was about to be quenched after decades, but it didn't mean as much to him as the woman at his side. Fate indeed played interesting tricks.

The ambassador still wore the raiment of his trade, if somewhat rumpled and askew. He doubtlessly had been mishandled during his removal from the Home

World but bore no visible injuries. Considerably older, his face worn and seamed, Rush maintained that shallow attempt at superiority he'd affected years ago when Vayne thought to use his daughter against the man. Perhaps not shallow to him, however, because Rush took his time getting to his feet and curled his lip at the sight of Vayne and his chosen.

The sovereign knew the instant Rush recognized Neira. The *paca* had probably served to give the impression of a Shadalla female until they moved closer to the holding cell. If he'd required additional confirmation he'd received it. Neira saw it too, her hand tensing for a brief moment as the color drained from the ambassador's lips.

"Ambassador." Vayne gave a brief nod.

Visibly trying to pull himself together, the other man wiped at his mouth with the back of one hand. "What is the meaning of this, Sovereign? This kidnapping."

"You are being transported to Nibiru. To face charges of genocide."

With a glance at Neira, Rush furrowed his brow. "I assure you, I have no idea of what you refer to. This is preposterous and—"

Vayne cut him off, tired of the charade. He'd indeed lost the taste for it now that the end was in sight. "Save your response for the trial, Ambassador. I find I'm not interested."

****

Evil hid behind many faces, or perhaps wore them blatantly if one had the wherewithal—or the inclination—to look. Neira stared at the weedy old man who quavered in the face of the accusation. He reminded her of a surface rat trying to find a way back to the safety of its burrow without leaving its spoils behind. But his voice reminded her of something else and if not for Vayne's reassuring and supportive presence she might have felt faint. The echo and flicker of horrible memories danced in some remote area of her brain but were easily dismissed. They weren't going to whisper to her anymore.

She didn't follow Home World politicians or their politics, although as a soldier she had done their bidding. One was the same as the other to those in the service. Don't wonder why. Do…or die. She dismissed that errant thought too. Neira hadn't laid eyes on this poor excuse for a human before but she'd heard him more than once, his voice unmistakable. Thin and with the undertone of bluster. Surface rat.

"Baraith threw you to the dogs." It was a calculated risk, but she took it.

Vayne went so still she wondered if he breathed, but Rush's attention was fixed on her. He opened and closed that petulant mouth and swallowed before replying. "If you're referring to the Juxtant Monarch, I've never met him and thus have no idea what you might be insinuating. And who might you be to speak thus to an ambassador?"

Ignoring his attempt to distract her, Neira spoke quickly. "It must have been difficult for you, wondering if I knew you were present on Ureses. Difficult for you to travel inconspicuously there, when he summoned you." She was guessing, but it made sense Baraith would use and blackmail anyone still alive that had been involved with the genetic weapon. And for sure he couldn't go to the Home World, being so easily recognized.

"I have no idea—"

"He has his own exit strategy, Mr. Ambassador. He put you in the sovereign's path to make it easier for him. Provide him some cover." Would he hear the lie?

Rush narrowed his beady eyes and she could almost hear his brain spinning. She tried one last time. "Don't you wonder how I ended up here? On this ship with the sovereign? Doesn't it seem strange—like a conspiracy? I would think you'd want to push back and take a little revenge of your own."

With a bitter sound that passed for a laugh, the man gestured at Vayne. "I'll see no mercy regardless."

"But you'll have the satisfaction that he isn't living a luxurious life while you're…not."

She put unobtrusive pressure on Vayne's arm, and he followed her lead and turned to escort her from the area. She fought disappointment when the ambassador didn't immediately respond, but better they kept up an act of indifference.

"He's closer than one would think. And he has a bold plan. I'd tell you if I knew more," Rush called out to them.

Vayne slowed their progress and moved his head to stare back at the ambassador, then spoke to the single guard. "Feed him and ensure he has access to a change of clothing."

Instead of returning to the cramped cabin, he walked her along to the lift. "Well done, little *leicat*."

The praise warmed her, although in truth they hadn't learned much. Baraith hadn't survived as long as he had, on the run, eluding both the hunters on the Home World and Vayne's, without cunning and resources. And he was known for his machinations. That warmth in her belly chilled to ice when she thought of bold plans and who might be aiding him.

They gained the bridge almost immediately, and she shadowed Vayne without a sound, feeling him process the little information Rush had provided. It was eerie how quickly she was learning to read him. *Like a soul mate.* After ushering her to a seat, he took the captain's chair and she watched as his crew brought him reports and made verbal additions in response to his questions. It appeared he'd called for reinforcements and they'd arrived and were now planning to run the blockade of Outriders between here and Nibiru. Neira hated the feeling of being helpless on a star vessel. She preferred to do her fighting face-to-face and hand-to-hand. As she brooded, it struck her how seamlessly she'd fit into Vayne's space—and when confronting Rush, Neira had thought of the sovereign as her lifemate.

Her previous anxiety and wariness had diminished considerably, replaced by a sense of calm acceptance. She glanced around and encountered not a few wistful stares, all with an undertone of what she interpreted as pride and excitement. It struck her she was now ranked as royalty and Neira wondered if she wanted the burden or if she could even shoulder it and do it justice. Vayne fixed her with a look and she returned it. The very air seethed and she cast off her worries in the face of such lust. The dampening of her underwear made her shift in her seat and the sovereign's eyes dilated, the ocean turquoise absorbed by the dark pupils. The others on the bridge vanished in her narrow vision. Her focus was entirely on Vayne, and she struggled to remember where she was and exercise some decorum.

Leaning forward, he muttered, "I want to become that cave male your people speak of, Neira. I wish to drag you back to our quarters and have my way with you. But duty calls and I must ask you to retire there, and wait. Our connection is distracting the crew."

Nodding, she shakily got to her feet, grateful one of them had some control. Maybe this was what came of a long sexual drought broken by amazing hotness and exceptional sex, but there was a time and a place. Her presence on the bridge had been calculated, she knew, and the message was received—bonded. Vayne was indeed a politician as well and knew how to make a statement, but now it was about maintaining discipline for the upcoming battle. So many roles, and her admiration grew. He rose with her and again offered his arm.

Such little time had passed, yet so much had transpired. Neira was distracted by Vayne's closeness once again in the narrow confines of the shaft. They stepped out and his hand drifted over her buttocks. Her soft underwear wasn't enough to contain her immediate response. The damp fabric flooded with her arousal and Vayne nearly dragged her to their quarters, his eyes wild and his gait awkward because of his erection.

He slammed his hand against the scanner and whirled her through the door as the panel hissed open. The *paca* was removed unceremoniously, the whisper of the fine fabric abrading her nipples and her senses. Vayne's strength mocked her height and healthy weight as he lifted her right off her feet and held her against the wall.

Neira registered the coolness of the hull until Vayne's mouth found hers and she heated past any boiling point. Wrapping her legs around his lean hips, she yanked him closer and the bulge in his pants pressed deliciously against her apex. She worked her pelvis against him, searching for just the right pressure on her clit.

Vayne chuckled and spoke against her lips. "I see we must learn to share control, little warrior."

She bit his bottom lip and soothed the mark with her tongue, her hands pressing against the back of his shoulders, one trailing upward to caress his nape. "You don't have a lot of time," she whispered.

"I have no time, yet I must find some, because I won't be able to function in this state." With a grunt he used his weight to pin her while freeing a hand to reach between them. Her panties were yanked to one side, the fabric twisting along the cleft of her buttocks and providing some interesting friction.

Before she could dwell on that, he released his cock and plunged inside of her without any fanfare. He was so big that she wondered if he'd fit, in that one thrust, but she was so wet he slid right in. This was the kind of sex she was familiar with, hurried, frantic couplings with both of them jockeying for position and control. Neira squeezed around him and he set his teeth in that tender join between shoulder and throat. Any familiarity then washed away at the bite of pain, followed by the furious pace he set. He held her in place effortlessly, powering through the thrusts and strokes, as an invader, a conqueror, and she found herself willingly submitting once again.

The way he moved put pressure where she needed it most. With more clever surges and a swivel of his hips her release built deep in her belly. She held on blindly, her fingers desperately clinging to him while knowing he'd never let her fall, and the orgasm blindsided her, eliciting a cry of completion that echoed in her ears. Vayne kept fucking her steadily, right through the vestiges of the climax, and she plateaued, hanging there in limbo until his strokes faltered.

Those big hands cupped her ass and tilted her, forcing him so deep it pinched like his teeth at her neck and she broke yet again, a shivery culmination that had her banging her head against the wall. Vayne instantly drew her off and stumbled to the bunk, Neira still wrapped around him.

He softened enough to give her some respite and

she feebly pushed at his chest in order to fill her lungs. He relaxed his hold and dropped a kiss on her forehead. "You make me wild, Neira."

Her nether parts were throbbing and she'd be sore when the endorphins faded, but for now she was soaking it all in. "Not complaining."

Standing, he rearranged his uniform, hiding that marvelous tool of her pleasure—better than all those inanimate ones stored in those drawers—and stared down at her. The passion had abated but Neira saw the other strong emotions reflected there and they scared her as much as drew her. She was experiencing something remarkably similar and all the sex and this feeling stuff was addling her brain.

"I must go and see to the negotiating. Unfortunately. If there is any to be done." His voice rasped over her much as his calloused hand had.

"Right. The negotiating." She shook her head a little and things cleared up. "Ah, right, you're going to use the ambassador as a bargaining chip for safe passage."

With an approving smile at her recollection, he nodded. "If necessary. Although I expect the appearance of four well-armed Shadalla warships will worry the Outriders enough. Especially when the chain of command has been interrupted."

"And better not to show your complete hand."

Vayne looked puzzled. "Oh, a card game reference. Indeed. You prove invaluable with your insights. Stay here, my love, until I come for you."

She absolutely didn't want him out of her sight but sucked it up. She was useless in this fight and would use the opportunity to play the role of his chosen. Female. Lifemate. Whatever. She belonged to him and he, to her. "All right."

"Such resignation," he teased. "But it's for the best."

"I know. It would be different on the battlefield."

That look tightened his features. A look that signaled there was no way in hell he'd allow her to fight by his side on any battlefield, and it was irksome. But it wasn't even in play and she wasn't wasting her energy. With an effort, she kept silent and he squinted, then gave her that smile that made her knees wobble. Such a *girl*. "We will never be bored in our relationship."

That was something they could agree on and she nodded. Vayne leaned in to kiss her and she shuddered with sudden premonition.

"What is it?"

"A feeling. I really don't know."

Studying her, he then shrugged. "I won't dismiss anything you feel, little warrior. I'll program the display panel for you to contact me if you need to."

That eased her mind and she mustered up a smile, taking the opportunity to kiss him before watching him leave once again. His satisfied smirk at her display of affection made her want to pinch him. This *thing* between them was going to take a lot of getting used to and she should probably work on her denial. Soul mate wasn't in her vocabulary but was the best descriptor if she allowed herself to think of it. Neira clambered to her feet and tugged her constricting underwear off, heading to wash up. She'd change into her tunic and leggings to make a point—if only to herself. *Lots* to get used to.

Chapter Ten

Calling on his self-control, Vayne took his chair on the bridge and put all thoughts of Neira aside—or as far aside as he could. His crew cast sidelong glances, then settled into their tasks. Leric updated him and he had brief conversations with the commanders of the other ships. He didn't know any of them well, but their records were exemplary, all of them, and he had full confidence they'd manage the Outriders without having to produce Rush.

"Take us out of the Falls, all necessary speed and in defense formation only." No sense in provoking the Home World ships.

"Sir." Leric ensured his commands were followed and the future began to unfold.

In a surprisingly short time, the helm reported the other ships within sensor range and they were hailed.

"Captain Franks. Home World. Permission to come on board." It was difficult to really tell anything from the other man's voice, but to Vayne it lacked certainty, even if the request was framed more as a demand.

The other three Shadalla ships were using the cover of the Falls to flank the Outriders—if all went well and Vayne's efforts were distracting enough.

Vayne identified himself, then denied Frank's request and asked the reasoning. "The Home World and the Shadalla have a treaty. Explain why you would presume to have the right to board us."

Upon ascertaining Vayne's rank and status, the other captain very obviously became flustered. "We have reason to believe you have a criminal on your ship. Perhaps someone who went aboard under false pretense."

So they were going that route. Not a rescue mission, then, cleverly avoiding any implication that the Shadalla were kidnapping human females and thus upping the ante. That woman—Toya—must have made a transmission. Vayne again refused and refuted the idea that he harbored any criminals, even if having the ambassador on board begged that assertion. They went back and forth, with the threats escalating on the Outrider captain's side and resolute resistance on his.

The other man closed the com and Vayne's crew increased their alert status. He wondered if the Outriders were seeking direction from the Home World and weren't receiving any, seeing as Vayne had the person ultimately directing them, in a cell on his vessel. He hoped they would withdraw, not wishing to threaten a treaty that had taken a very long time to negotiate.

"Sovereign?" Captain Franks finally hailed again and it actually made Vayne start, the tension so thick that the air on the bridge felt difficult to inhale.

"Captain?"

"Accept our apologies. We are withdrawing. An error."

Keeping his reaction under control, Vayne gravely acknowledged the other man and listened as his helmsmen reported that the Outriders were grouping in an apparent flight formation. He was at the end of a long exhale when weapons fire was reported.

Leaping to his feet, he barked out a demand for clarification even as his helmsman took evasive action.

"Not sure, sir." Leric frantically worked his panel. "One of our ships fired on an Outrider!"

Chaos reigned in the next several stints as his ship withdrew to the Falls at highest possible speed and the others withdrew on his orders, giving the Outriders a wide berth. The battle was over almost as soon as it began, thanks to the lack of combatants and the apparent reluctance of the Outriders to pursue, now that they realized Vayne's ship wasn't alone. The *Tomodr* escaped any fire, but two of the other ships weren't as lucky. Fortunately there were no fatalities, but one cruiser was crippled and an evacuation was in order, leaving only a skeleton crew on board in deference to the damaged life support. The Outriders sustained minimal damage, something Captain Franks conveyed when Vayne again made contact. Leric had advised there'd been an accidental firing from one of those ships, and Vayne ordered an investigation.

"An accidental firing, Captain. We'll be happy to make recompense for damages. Send the information to our embassy on the Home World."

With a sharp comment about untrained crew and trigger happy individuals, the captain led the rest of the Home World ships in the direction of Earth. The Shadalla bided their time until certain they were once again alone in this area of space.

"Orders, sir?"

"See to it that the other captains arrange for the crew of the disabled ship to be distributed amongst the others and a salvage operation organized. And have the hunters return to pick up Rush, take him to Nibiru. We'll escort him but I don't want him on *Tomodr*." Especially now that he didn't need him. "The others can stay behind to shelter the disabled ship."

Vayne really didn't need to issue any of those orders, other than the one concerning the ambassador. His military were all well trained—despite some idiot's accidental weapon discharge—but he wanted to reinstate his control. It was unnecessary in truth, but nothing about this mission had been without its twists and turns. Without waiting for Leric's confirmation, he took his leave and went to await the hunters, knowing Rush would be at the boarding dock shortly. He paused only to contact Neira and give her a summary of the events. The relief in her voice and her heartfelt if halting expressions of support made him even more determined to return to her as soon as he rid his ship of a certain vermin.

The contingent of hunters that boarded the *Tomodr* consisted of three males, all fit and combat toughened, if their cocky attitudes were anything to go by. One was even taller than the rest, an amazing specimen, indeed. He sported heavy bandages around his face, nearly concealing his features. He looked strangely familiar regardless, but Vayne was distracted by the arrival of Rush, who protested bitterly as he was towed along by one of the loading dock crew. He made a mental note to find out the wounded hunter's identity and offer recompense.

"Sovereign?" Leric spoke at his shoulder, having joined him under the cover of the ambassador's futile rhetoric. "You're required on the bridge for a transmission."

"Have them relay it here," he said irritably. He wanted to oversee Rush's transfer.

"It's coded."

With an abrupt nod, he strode away, but not before telling Leric to keep the ambassador in place until he returned. Upon gaining the bridge, he determined the message was indeed coded, and puzzling. Annis was dead. Murdered. No lingering, unpleasant death for him, but a quick one, immediately after the hunter had delivered him to the ghetto. The fine hair on the nape of his neck lifted as he considered what might have transpired. Shaking his head, knowing he'd wait for answers, he made his way back to where Rush waited, the confines of the lift a burden on his senses.

He stepped out at the boarding dock—and into chaos. Rush's slight form lay sprawled and bloody, the body of a hunter slumped beside him, his head battered misshapen. A second hunter clasped a bad gut wound, his back against the hull. Leric was defending himself against the bandaged warrior, the body of Vayne's crew member near his feet. Vayne freed his blade and rushed forward on a roar, but he distracted Leric, who caught a vicious slash across the shoulder as a result. A great spray of blood accompanied the injury and his exec wobbled, then collapsed.

Blinded by the crimson wash of Leric's blood, the big, bandaged male was easily brought down by a hard blow to the temple from the butt of Vayne's knife, crashing to the floor in a loose welter of limbs. Vayne was already ripping a sleeve from his uniform and attempting to staunch his exec's wound. An artery had been severed and a tourniquet had to be applied in an extremely difficult place. The coms were down, so that meant getting his friend stabilized and to medical on his watch alone. He worked frantically, his hands wet and slippery with the other male's hot blood.

****

Neira's query to the bridge was initially met with silence before Eltrast identified himself. "The sovereign is overseeing the transfer of the prisoner, my lady."

Thanking him, she considered. The battle was over, with the Outriders discouraged and heading home. If it hadn't been for that undisciplined shot someone had taken there wouldn't have even been a battle—skirmish, as Vayne termed it in their very brief conversation. It had caused her concern, regardless, for she hated feeling impotent, not to mention this unsettled feeling that persisted. Paranoia should be a thing of her past. She wanted, no, *needed*, to see Vayne, and wasn't content to merely hear from him.

Deciding it would be okay for her to see Rush transferred, she ran her hands over her tunic and leggings. Vayne was clearly serious about keeping her naked and she was lucky her clothes weren't rags. Another thing to discuss and reach a compromise on, because while the sex was amazing and she wouldn't turn it down, this whole naked thing was over the top. Although it did mean they could get right down to it. She laughed at her transparency. Vayne wouldn't be after her all the time once the initial draw wore off. She couldn't imagine when that might be, however, if he felt as strongly about consummating their union as she did. Often and thoroughly.

On impulse, she snatched out her *palka* and her blade, tucking the latter into her boot and stroking the polished wood of her favored weapon. She didn't question the need to arm herself while trying to dismiss the discomfort in her belly. Maybe Vayne would agree to some sparring before they got underway, to bleed off her anxiety that had mounted as she waited. The horizontal exercise was one thing, but she needed to pair her body with her brain and sparring with her sovereign would do the trick.

The crew were going about their business, and all gave her respectful nods, most accompanied by a slightly raised brow. She wasn't supposed to be wandering around without Vayne, but surely that was just on his planet. His crew were disciplined individuals and with the recent *skirmish* had enough to occupy their time, standing down and checking systems and all. She might not understand starships but battles were battles and the aftermath required examining and securing weapons, tending to any injuries, debriefing and the like. That was how they got better at what they did.

Gaining the lift, she took it to the boarding deck, a sense of anticipation and that little lick of worry niggling at her. She would probably disappoint Vayne by leaving their quarters unescorted, she decided, hence the concern, but it was too late. The door hissed open and a nightmare unfolded.

Her sovereign was crouched over the prostrate form of a crew member, a red trail of blood all around him. Four other bodies lay in the unmistakable posture of death, like a child's carelessly discarded figurines. Rush was one of them. Her reality unfolded in slow motion as her vision narrowed on the bandaged male moving swiftly toward Vayne, who had raised his head to look in her direction, no doubt drawn by the sound of the lift.

"Your six!" Her scream of warning caused Vayne to jerk from his stance but not enough to put any effective distance between him and the descending blade that pierced his back. The blow slammed it in to the hilt. Then it was withdrawn and raised to strike again as her lifemate's big body stiffened and crumpled on top of the man he had been ministering to.

Muscle memory kicking in, Neira whipped the *palka* at that hand gripping the knife. It smashed with resounding effect, pulling a yowl of pain and fury from the big male before rebounding and bouncing across the floor in her direction. She ran to scoop it up and face her opponent over Vayne's still form. The floor was littered with the dead and she wished she could risk a check of her sovereign's pulse. Because surely he wasn't one of them. That would be too much for her to bear, worse than anything she'd experienced in her life. Her belly clenched hard and she fought to stay focused on the enemy.

Cradling his injured hand in his other, the alien male straightened to his full height. She couldn't make out his features, shrouded as they were by the field bandages utilized when the medics with all their technology weren't immediately available. Old school. Her battle senses calmed her as she assessed the situation, setting Vayne's predicament aside for now. He wasn't dead. He wasn't. But help was two decks up and the alien was between her and the only exit—and the com was smashed. *Do or die, Neira.*

"So, we come full circle, pet."

The voice called to her terror, asleep and sated because she'd felt so safe and protected—owned—by Vayne, and it stirred uneasily like a snake waking in a burrow. *Baraith.* She tasted the name and the foulness of it soured her mouth. A strange and deadly calm descended over her as her lifemate died at her feet, the pumping of his precious blood slowing to a trickle. As it ebbed, something in her own chest shriveled, to be replaced by a terrible sensation of cold. Neira edged to one side and took a stance. Baraith cast a look at Vayne and sneered.

"I thought I would find him on Nibiru while in my new appearance. It would have been more difficult to slay him there, so once again fate has intervened. Always for me." He flexed his hand, the fingers misshapen and swollen. His eyes narrowed on her, now the same surprising shade of blue Vayne's had boasted, the pupils lacking the Juxtant trait. But it was Baraith. "What are you to him, Neira Grekov? Bodyguard? Mistress? *Pet?*"

"His chosen." She said it with pained pride and watched with muted satisfaction as Baraith's astonishment kept him silent. Just not for long.

Glee replaced the incredulity and the bastard capered in place, gloating. "Revenge is indeed so sweet."

"Too bad you won't have much time to enjoy it." Neira followed her assertion with a sudden move over Vayne that brought her well within Baraith's reach. As she thought, he didn't expect it as he sadistically savored her proclamation, and the blow she dealt his leg took him down, the kneecap shattered and mangled through his uniform pants.

She danced away, taking care not to slip on the blood or trip on the bodies, because she needed to finish this before the emptiness in her chest and the barely contained screaming in her brain incapacitated her. Baraith could conceivably take over the ship with his experience and resourcefulness if he got away, to wreak havoc. He might even get to Nibiru, because he didn't even look like himself anymore, hiding in plain sight. But she knew.

Someone moaned and she shot a look toward the man Vayne had been helping. Leric. Oh God. Victoria. The distraction almost cost her, but Baraith couldn't have known how much a ruined kneecap hurt and his hiss of pain as he attempted to stealthily rise and step to her was enough of an alert to keep her distance. She watched for another opportunity, and when he reached behind him to free another blade, snatched out her own and lunged. His upper body was covered in light armor, negating a killing strike, so she buried the point deep in Baraith's upper thigh.

He howled, then made a guttural sound as she dragged her knife back out, slicing along the length of his leg. The outpouring of blood gave her hope—she might have slashed an artery, and if so he would bleed out. But she'd entered his space, and his injured hand swung hard and caught her face, thudding against the cheekbone. She rolled away from the impact, losing the knife in the process. Her retreat helped to mitigate the damage, but the vision in that eye immediately clouded. *Orbital floor fracture.* Neira choked back a pained groan as she catalogued the injury and scrambled another few feet.

Baraith wobbled on his injured legs, unable to put any real weight on his knee, and clearly in pain as a result of the stab wound to his right thigh.

But he was still dangerous. "You're running out of maneuvering room, pet. The Juxtant heal quickly, even from injuries such as these." He was using that mesmerizing voice on her, the one he'd employed when he soothed Alexi, tricking him into believing it was all over, building cruel hope before inflicting more creative torture. But the damage she'd exacted interfered with his tone, adding another layer, and she was able to resist him.

"You won't come back from the dead." She barely recognized her voice, flat and barren of any inflection. It didn't matter what happened to her but she had to stop him.

He leered at her, one now black soulless eye as hypnotic as a snake, only far more dangerous—what had to be a contact lens still shrouded the other in that vibrant blue. He threw his blade in a sweeping underhand. She caught the movement and lurched sideways, hampered by the nausea and dizziness resulting from the head injury, and the knife, meant for her gut, pierced her side. It hurt like the furies of hell, an almost welcome reprieve from the crippling sense of loss she could no longer hold at bay. *Vayne.*

Blinking, trying to find a way to exacerbate his collapse before her own, Neira feinted with the *palka*, ignoring the agony in her ribs. When her foe lowered his fists to block her, she whipped her cherished weapon upward, at his face. The polished wood made a resounding *whack* as it cracked Baraith's forehead, and the impact shuddered the *palka* from her hand. It fell to his feet. Neira desperately reached for it, grunting at the effort, and the polished piece of wood slipped into her grasp. The room stank of coppery death and freshly spilled blood, and warm liquid ran down her side to saturate her leggings. She had to get this done before he outlasted her and concocted some story to explain the slaughter.

His uninjured hand rose to strip away the bandages and despite her flawed vision, Neira took the sight in, unable to swallow back her reaction. Baraith smiled, his huge body weaving in front of her as he balanced on one foot.

"We're cousins, pet." He suddenly flinched and she wondered if it hurt him to speak, if she'd managed more than a concussion. She wouldn't let herself accept his appearance. How like *Vayne* he appeared. Her belly knotted in on itself and forced bile up her throat as he continued, "And the Home World has remarkable reconstructive surgeons when one has the right connections."

"No." She couldn't voice anything else and dropped into the fighting mode she'd trained in for years and years, the pain of her injuries fading away. She had the impression of taking Baraith by surprise once again as she drove herself forward, using her strong legs, wielding the weapon of her native land with precision and accuracy.

As she drove him back, she knew she did more damage to that travesty of a face, his nose crunching beneath her fevered blows, and thought she might have landed a telling one on his temple before he had her by the throat. His huge hand wrapped around her neck, a brutal parody of the way her lifemate had gripped her with possession and love. Vertebrae creaked and she had a sense of flying before everything went black.

****

Vayne nearly screamed with pain when hands lifted him and moved him to a flat surface. He knew it was urgent that he attend to something but the agony was crippling, like a burning steel rod was stuck in his back. Drawing a full breath was difficult, but if he concentrated, it became a little more orchestrated, as though his brain was short-circuiting commands if he rushed. He hadn't felt like this since—

Someone moaned—a male, and that someone was placed beside him. Vayne peered at him, barely turning his head, unable to lift it for a better look.

"…survivors. Thought we had another but his brain must have been scrambled because he seized and then expired. Massive blows to the head and a knee. Stab wounds. Nothing to be done."

The sovereign recognized that voice above him. Stenlor. He tried to clear his throat but managed only a cough of sound.

"Sovereign?" Stenlor crouched beside him to make eye contact. Although with the way Vayne was lying he could only see the man out of one eye. It was disconcerting and his beast railed against the weakness. He coughed again in acknowledgment and pain lanced through his chest.

"You must remain completely still. You took a blade to a heart. No exit wound. We don't want the bleeding to start again."

Decades of war, fighting, and the only injury he'd sustained during that time was the stab wound that badly injured one of his hearts. And now, a second such injury. He blinked his eye in agreement and Stenlor apparently understood.

"Whoever applied the tourniquet saved your exec, sir. We'll take you both to sick bay shortly."

"Anyone else?" He managed to whisper the question, because there was a traitor on his ship, the injured hunter.

His medic hesitated and Vayne cursed his enforced immobility. "Stenlor."

"There is a dead human and three dead hunters, and the landing bay crew member responsible for the area has also faded, sir. It's a bloodbath. I've never seen the like aside from hand-to-hand on the field."

He felt surprisingly better, knowing the traitor was accounted for—dead—and elated that he'd saved Leric. He knew he'd deal with the loss of his crew member and the loyal hunters later and want to unravel the mystery of the traitor, but for now he was focused on the living. Something chewed at the edge of memory, something about the attack, but he couldn't recall... "Don't tell my chosen. Not until I've been stitched, whatever, and ready for release." His order came out in bits and pieces of gravelly monologue.

"No, sir. I won't tell her." Stenlor's voice was hoarse to Vayne's ears, hardly the cool scientist. Perhaps he was worse off than he thought, and he prepared himself. No, he couldn't die, couldn't be that gravely injured. He'd only just found her...Neira.

Stenlor's orders precluded any further conversing. The transfer to medical was excruciating, the lift being so narrow he was propped upright, and also because the medic was reluctant to administer pain medication until his heart issue could be better assessed. Vayne thought it might well burst from his chest when the pain made it thunder in his ears, despite Stenlor's continual reassurances.

The cool, antiseptic air of the medical bay soothed his senses and, now on a medical cot, still on his belly, Vayne suffered the prodding and poking of Stenlor's trade. Physicians. They administered pain without apology for the greater good. His medic stepped away with a satisfied grunt. Leric's pale face came into Vayne's narrow viewpoint, his exec stretched out on the next cot. He was to have been moved first at Vayne's insistence but apparently Stenlor outranked his sovereign. Leric looked well under the blanket of a dose of numbing drugs, and while he was glad the male wasn't in pain, Vayne was envious.

A static sound filled the air around him as Stenlor oversaw the test to determine Vayne's heart damage, and after an eternity the medic crouched to face his sovereign.

"Your heart is destroyed—the one that suffered the previous damage. It pumped out considerable blood volume before your other heart asserted itself. Prevented total exsanguination. I'm going to remove the affected organ and seal the wound and you'll receive a sedative for the process."

Impatient and in discomfort, Vayne grunted. "Get on with it, then."

"Is the pain diminishing? You are quite coherent."

"I thought someone was standing on my chest and driving their heel and their sword into my sternum. That feeling isn't so prominent now." Thank the gods of Isord.

"That would be your other heart assuming the total responsibility for maintaining circulation, Sovereign. Powering your body. I've read studies that cite such a process and it is recorded as being excruciating."

"Then perhaps it's a good thing I was out for a while," Vayne gritted out. Scientists and their case studies. Physicians and pain. And Stenlor was all in one, something the sovereign was extremely grateful for.

The laparoscopic removal of the destroyed heart went quickly, utilizing the stab wound, with Stenlor giving him a synthetic blood transfusion during the process. The medic detailed his every move but Vayne felt nothing, despite being wide awake, his Shadalla abilities already promoting fast healing. Stenlor cautioned him and insisted that he rest for more stints than he cared for. But he didn't want to upset Neira any more than he had to, so grudgingly obeyed. She would be wondering where he'd gotten to, and that too was bothersome. Stenlor agreed to relay an excuse, busy with his tasks.

Eltrast was summoned to make a full report and fill in the holes. Vayne was grateful that his medic had insisted he rest and allow both his own physiology and modern medicine to heal him. He knew Rush had been murdered, had seen two of his hunters and a crew dead or dying and his exec fighting for his life. He even had a dim memory of subduing the bandaged hunter with a blow before administering to Leric. It was the information Eltrast shared about the traitor that sucker punched him.

"Juxtant? You're certain?"

"The facial reconstruction would have misled anyone, sir. The Shadalla and the Juxtant are closely related, as you know. It was his eyes that gave him away. A contact had been dislodged in the fight and his identity was obvious. Juxtant. Stenlor advises we should have his identity from his RNA shortly." Eltrast shuffled and looked away.

"I'm thoroughly sick of having my crew crouch and talk to me as I lie on my belly, Eltrast. Do me the courtesy of a complete report rather than me dragging the details from you. What aren't you saying?"

Three beats. "He looks like you, sir. With additional surgery and the right color of ocular implants he would *be* you. Same size and weight. Identical in appearance."

He'd delay his conclusion until the RNA results were in, Vayne decided, despite the fact he'd already made the leap with certainty in his gut. The imposter had been Baraith. But if the Juxtant Monarch had been on the

Home World all this time, surrounding himself with allies, calling in his favors…the treaty be damned. Heads would roll. His brain ticked over and wondered how the other hunters had been persuaded to accept him as one of their own, because Baraith was on that vessel that brought Rush to the *Tomodr*. Rush. The ambassador was responsible for more than he thought. It was highly unfortunate the man was dead. He considered how things had likely unfolded.

Hunters were solitary and though communicated regularly, they came together as necessary, so Baraith could have dispatched one and assumed his identity. Hence the bandages for the trip to the *Tomodr*. The monarch would have been privy to all of Vayne's dispatches. That Annis had met his premature fate at Baraith's machinations if not his own hand was a foregone conclusion. The councilman couldn't spill secrets from a dead mouth. Then the Juxtant Monarch had come here. Was he the one who'd fired on the Outriders? To precipitate another incident? As Vayne worked it through, the machines monitoring his recovery beeped an alarm and Stenlor hustled over.

"Sovereign, you need to calm yourself. Your system is adapting but stress will impede the process."

"Do you have the results yet?" Vayne drew in deep breaths, ignoring the tiny tearing sensations in his chest. He didn't need results, but the others would. He'd reached his own conclusions and didn't expect any surprises.

"No. But soon." Stenlor would know what he was asking. He'd have had more time to put the pieces together. Because *he* hadn't been out of commission, bleeding out on the deck of the landing bay, stabbed in the back—

"Who stabbed me?" His voice was powerful again

and brooked no subterfuge.

Stenlor didn't flinch. "I had time only to do a cursory assessment based on rudimentary forensics. I've been…busy."

Vayne closed his eyes, waiting.

"I believe it was the Juxtant. He was the last to fade."

"I put him on the deck with a blow to the head while I attended Leric." The least he could do after distracting his exec in the struggle, and he was elated Baraith was dead at last—even if he'd have preferred to have dealt the final blow. "He must have revived enough to take advantage of my back to him." The Juxtant always were cowardly fighters and Baraith was no exception.

"That would explain it, sir." Eltrast had fine beads of sweat on his upper lip and still couldn't meet Vayne's stare.

"Roll me over."

Stenlor grimaced but stood, and between him and Eltrast got Vayne turned over onto his back. A number of pillows helped him sit and once he powered past the ache just above his sternum, he could breathe again. He pinned the medic with a look that usually had grown males bowing and scraping. "Who do I have to thank for killing him, then?" he rasped.

The way Stenlor's face paled actually sent a frisson of dread up Vayne's spine. The other male's eyes slammed shut, then opened. "Your chosen."

So one heart *wasn't* up to the task of supporting his body, just as he had thought earlier, after bonding with Neira. He clung to consciousness with a tenacity that surprised even him, resisting the swirling dark that threatened to swallow up his struggling brain. His little warrior had faced Baraith, alone. There were other scenarios available to him as his memory returned—the bodies strewn about as he lay incapacitated, unable to defend her. The com smashed and no hope of rescue as she threw down with a male double her body weight and with a reach that—

"Sovereign. Calm yourself and heal." The alarms cut through his stupor and he blinked at Stenlor.

"Where is she?" The question forced itself past his throat, slicing like razor blades with a garnish of terror.

Stenlor moved sideways and gestured. Vayne followed the motion and his eyes took in the sight of his little warrior, lying still and silent, just beyond his reach. All that was visible was her pale face and ebony hair, both blending in and a stark contrast to the white of the pillow. The medic and Eltrast foiled his attempt to leap from the cot and go to her, and Vayne thought of public whippings and beheadings before turning to Stenlor.

Anticipating his questions, the other male said, "Your chosen has sustained multiple injuries. Broken bones, specifically her right ulna and a cracked shoulder blade—a fracture of the orbital floor and a stab wound to the side of her abdomen. The blade struck her ribs and deflected, missing any major organs, but she lost a great deal of blood. She was also choked and two vertebrae in her neck showed twisting fractures."

"Prognosis?" There was no inflection in his tone, matching Stenlor's matter-of-fact report. Because if Vayne allowed his emotions to color his voice the chances were he'd be in lockdown to protect the crew. The need to reincarnate Baraith and tear him apart and into tiny, unrecognizable pieces made him tremble, and the ache in his chest expanded to dizzying proportions.

"I repaired the fractures and I detected no brain damage from the blow to the face. But the blood loss…"

Stenlor straightened and squared his shoulders. "I gave her a blood substitute, sparingly. Shadalla and humans are compatible but there are some differences in platelets. I was worried about her throwing a clot. However, there have been no adverse effects."

When the male hesitated, Vayne narrowed his eyes and waited, certain the worst was yet to come.

"She will not wake up! And is fading. I'm sorry, sir. I don't understand it. At first I thought it was because of your injury. For all intents and purposes it should have been fatal and was incapacitating in that moment. But she clearly fought the Juxtant to the death, and I can't believe she would have had the strength if her life was tied to yours. And you didn't fade!"

Looking longingly over at Neira, who breathed so shallowly the sheet covering her barely moved, Vayne had a thought. "Is she…with child? Did the fight…"

"No. Not pregnant. That was something I checked immediately before I healed her." Stenlor laughed, a sound empty of mirth. "I healed her but she won't wake up. Sovereign, we treated her first, before even you—our ruler. Committed treason."

"Because you knew of my wishes had I been able to command." Truly, Vayne had surrounded himself with remarkable males on this voyage.

"She is your future, sir."

Ignoring how that fact hurt him worse that his adapting heart, and cursing his weakness, Vayne used his right to command. "Move her closer. Beside me."

Her cot tucked beside his, he scrutinized her features. "She is a true warrior."

Stenlor snorted. "Indeed. That Juxtant was severely injured. I'll catalogue his injuries for you."

Vayne didn't care and blocked out the chatter as he noted the bruising on his little warrior's beautiful face.

It was the only thing visible to denote such terrible trauma, and even that was fading as a result of his medic's technological skill. Neira was cold to the touch and he carefully tested his strength, sitting up and reaching to tug at her.

"Allow me, sir." The medic didn't question his sovereign's intent but intuited it and eased Neira's slender form over until she fit up against Vayne. So still and cold, yet she molded against him as though it had always been her rightful place. Eltrast muttered about returning to duty and hurried away, his face strained and anxious. Vayne hoped he would deviate and check in on his own chosen. One never knew when fate would intervene.

As his strength returned and his body stabilized, Vayne worked the sheets free and held his chosen closer. Skin to skin, he held her and stroked her pale face, pressing his lips against hers. The faint huff of her breath gave him hope and he clung to it, grimly. He spoke her name over and over, using his body heat in an attempt to warm her, and prayed. Stenlor went away to finish his work after a baffled look at Neira, and she and Vayne huddled together in a mockery of the intimacy they had so recently established.

Chapter Eleven

"Neira. Neira! Little warrior." Vayne's urgent voice echoed above her but she was down so deep, so far, that she couldn't respond. Did the Shadalla believe in the afterlife? Did lifemates fade and find the other later? So many things she didn't know and hadn't had the time to ask. They'd had so little time, thanks to her stupid issues. She wanted to believe she could talk with him, even here, but there was no comfort when one lost the love of their life, and it didn't seem possible she would be so blessed.

So cold. She was back to feeling chilled again, frozen to the marrow. If she didn't think about Vayne dying at her feet while she was powerless to aid him, perhaps this abyss would swallow her and afford her the kindness of oblivion. But perhaps her penance was to remain here, cold for eternity.

Drifting, she ignored the increasing desperation in that voice. His voice.

One would think one's life might flash before one but not here, so she sought it out. She summoned up memories of her childhood, the sweet, smiling faces of her sisters, Anika and Izabella, making her own lips twitch and curve. A single tear formed as she mourned them, separated so many years ago. Her parents—hard working, tough Russian stock, also gone, missing in the war. The military had served as Neira's home and became her family. Again, all gone, lost. Perhaps if it hadn't been for the reawakening of her heart and healing of her soul by the alien male who'd kidnapped her, yet made her his own without the advantages he'd originally touted, she might rest easy in this state of limbo. But clearly, she'd suffer for eternity, so she might as well get on with it. She wouldn't dwell on the last moments of Vayne's life, not the way she'd watched his big, strong body fade. Instead, she would keep the memory of his beloved face right in the forefront of her mind, open and vulnerable as he allowed her into his very being.

Whispers of sensation chased themselves across her cheeks and gentle touches pressed against her closed lids. More sweet pressure and warmth on her mouth as her body warmed and melted against something heated. It was the worst form of torture as once again his voice spoke her name and the sound eddied around her. Not limbo, then, but hell. Tantalized and tormented. She whimpered and heard the noise echo like a small animal, trapped and afraid. Her pathetic struggles were subdued and denied—then soothed. Neira begged...*please...noooo...* He was gone and how was she to exist like this?

"Neira. Enough. Your sovereign must insist. I command you to come back to me."

Again, she struggled, one arm flailing while her feet shuffled as if swaddled in sand. *Please.*

"I have you, little warrior. I have you. You're safe and in my arms. Let me hold you, keep you warm."

Bands of steel imprisoned her yet kept her in place against the directionless drifting, and the warmth was truly delicious. She dared relax infinitesimally and was rewarded with a pleased murmur that ruffled the hair at her temple. A deep breath to ease her angst filled her nostrils with Vayne's distinct, earthy scent. Startled, she blinked her eyes open.

Worried turquoise pools fringed with dark lashes stared down at her, drawing her heart and soul from the abyss, and his name flooded up her throat. "Vayne?"

"I'm here. Here with you, my chosen." His voice was hoarse with bubbling emotion.

"Are we dead?" The space was bright and filled

with sounds she knew well. Hospital sounds. She couldn't tear her gaze from his to orient herself.

A pained chuckle escaped him, and her breasts were compressed as his chest swelled. So close—and skin to skin. "We aren't dead, Neira. Although we should be, considering what has transpired."

"We're in sick bay," she guessed.

"We are. I despaired of you ever waking."

That was intriguing. She hadn't thought she was merely asleep. "We're naked. In sick bay. And you were dead. I saw you die." *Baraith!* Panic welled and only with a huge effort did she keep from flailing about in terror. She couldn't hurt Vayne.

"Shh, Neira. Breathe. You're safe."

"But he stabbed you—"

"And he is dead. I have survived, as have you." The relief was indescribable to know Baraith was dead.

She hung on every word as Vayne explained his survival, intensely grateful for the difference in Shadalla physiology. Cautiously, she gained a few inches in distance, pressing backward, and studied his chest.

"The injury in my back has healed, or nearly so," he offered, "and this time with no scarring, thanks to having the technology available."

"Are you…" She didn't know how to ask if he was going to be the same or struggle in later life. Heart transplants on the Home World were common if one had the money, and the success rate was very high, but… Not that it mattered. She'd take care of him, see that he took care.

"I'm fine. Without pain at all now and Stenlor assures me I won't know the difference once I conclude my recovery period. Unlike my crew member, the loyal hunters, and very nearly Leric. You know the ambassador was also killed. And you evidently saved my life from a traitor who was a Juxtant in disguise."

Neira was vastly relieved to hear that Leric would survive, and she spared a thought and a prayer for the dead, aside from Rush and Baraith. She pretended not to hear that her sovereign believed she'd saved him. It was simply too much to handle at the moment. She knew she'd have a private discussion with the medic regardless of Vayne's reassurances about his health and ruefully conceded she was going to become one of those women, the ones who worried and fussed over their—husbands. Her breathing increased exponentially as she thought the word and Vayne touched a finger to the pulse near her throat, his expression anxious.

"What is it? Are you dismayed because of that Juxtant?"

How could she say it? What words should she use? She'd informed Baraith that Vayne was her lifemate, she his chosen, and it had felt totally right in that moment. They were bonded and losing him had nearly killed her. Could she go through that again? Could she not?

"Neira. Turn to me. Please."

She snuggled into him and tucked her head beneath his chin. He stroked her back and she felt his cock harden and fill against her belly.

"Ignore that," he muttered. "You have only to touch me and I'm hard."

When she spoke, her words were muffled, but he'd said the Shadalla had excellent hearing, and she couldn't look at him yet. "I can't imagine life without you. I told…the Juxtant…you were my husband. It was Baraith, Vayne."

A finger slipped beneath her chin and he tilted her head back, moving so he could lock gazes. He didn't look surprised and his words underscored it. He was so intelligent, her husband, and had clearly been thinking things through while she was drifting in limbo. "You knew it was him. I can only imagine your…yet you prevailed. And you nearly faded when you thought I was lost to you, and you would still claim me as yours? Take that risk again?"

Forcing a tremulous smile, she nodded. "There's a price to pay for what you have given me and what you promise, and I'll pay it."

"Is there nothing that can defeat you, little warrior? Not the war, not the loss of family, not that time with the Juxtant and then how your own people treated you? Kidnapped and forced to fight for your life against the very Juxtant who was at the center of it all?" Vayne stared deep into her eyes. "I stand in awe of you, my chosen."

"I nearly didn't come back to you," she said quietly. "And if you hadn't called me, I wouldn't have."

"Then my prayers weren't in vain. And rest assured I'll keep that promise, little warrior. I owe you my life."

"And I owe you my soul."

****

As Neira dropped her head back onto his chest, Vayne's entire being exploded with joy. Like a beautifully forged blade, his chosen's bond with him had remained strong and true, regardless of the fact she was human and he was Shadalla. She cared for him so much that she preferred death if she lost him, however, and that would never do. He would give her much to live for, and once blessed with children things would work out differently should he have the misfortune to fade before her. It could indeed be misfortune, for, as sovereign, there were risks and rewards. High profile figures tended to draw attention both positive and negative, but he'd long accepted that fact and guarded against it.

His joy fizzled at the thought of losing her first, as would most likely happen because of their bodies' predetermined longevity, and his brain scrambled to compile all the reasons why that might not have to be so. Technology had a way of outstripping mortality. And he couldn't allow himself to think that way. Neira had withstood so many losses and deserved that he be equally resilient. One must live in the moment and experience everything. The silk of Neira's body against his own coarser skin reminded him of that point.

"Sovereign." Stenlor approached, a scanning device in his hand and information written across his features. At Vayne's nod he ran the small instrument over Neira and made satisfied sounds. "All vital signs are normal. Slightly elevated body temperature but I expect that's from—in any event she is fine. As healthy as yourself."

Ignoring the flush on the medic's face, Vayne asked, "And the RNA results?"

"Sir. I ran them three times against our data base. The Juxtant on our ship was Monarch Baraith."

His arms automatically tightened around Neira as the foul name fell from Stenlor's mouth in an unnecessary yet necessary confirmation. Did she remember that fight to the death or was she lacking in details as he had been when he came back to the land of the living? Vayne wanted to ask her what happened, debrief her, but hesitated when she disregarded the contention she had saved his life. How much could one woman handle?

Neira wiggled free of his protective grasp, holding the sheet against her breasts as she surveyed Stenlor. "But he's really dead, right?"

"Most assuredly, My Lady Sovereign. As you

humans say, as a doornail." The male looked bemused and glanced at Vayne.

"I just wasn't sure he would die because I blacked out when he—" She bit off her next words and looked away from him.

"Stenlor told me what he did to you. And what you did to him." Grim satisfaction colored his tone as he voiced the latter.

"As long as he's gone. He seemed…immortal. I didn't want him to somehow gain control of the *Tomodr*. And he had to pay for what he did to you."

Vayne waved Stenlor away and lowered his voice for her ears alone. "I do owe you my life, little warrior. Again, I stand in awe. And you faced your worst nightmare."

"And won," she said grimly, again clearly disregarding how indebted he was to her, but he'd ensure she never regretted it.

"I understand he…that is to say, Baraith had been altered to resemble me."

"Don't you say that. Don't you ever say that," she said, so fiercely the strong resemblance to a *leicat* was highly pronounced. "He is nothing like you. Nothing."

He soothed her, stroking over her back and arms until she settled. "We have come full circle, Neira. I have my beloved chosen, and other Shadalla males can follow my lead, now that we understand the opportunities."

"And no more stealing women." There was total inflexibility in that statement.

"No more stealing women," he agreed. "Although I'd do it again if it meant finding you."

Neira said nothing. Last word. Vayne smiled to himself.

Epilogue

Neira crept down the hall toward the room she and Vayne shared for sleeping—and other, more pleasurable pursuits. He denied her nothing, except this. He insisted on their own personal space, one that the children weren't allowed to breach, despite how she often longed to welcome them here. Perhaps when they were older, she mused, even though it was unlikely. Her sovereign loved his offspring with a depth of emotion she recognized, because he loved her with the same intensity, but he'd drawn the boundary and she'd respect it. His need for her was huge and never flagged.

Nibiru was now her home, and the house she shared with Vayne and their children, along with an astonishing number of primarily male Shadalla, was everything she could have hoped for. The city itself was clean and all the buildings well constructed from stone from the local quarries. The air quality was far better than that on the Home World, and the Shadalla were eons ahead in their respect for the environment. The countryside was peppered with efficient farming enterprises, and the factories were under stringent environmental controls. The Shadalla insisted on being self-sufficient in all matters—the result of near genocide. Some trade was allowed but only items that were deemed a necessity and couldn't be produced on Nibiru. Change was carefully considered and took a very long time.

Pausing for a moment to peer out the window in the hallway, she studied the rolling landscape, quite similar to that of her planet of birth, illuminated by Nibiru's two moons. The golden glow was shot with silver and she could make out the movements of the guards among the gardens. There were risks and dangers even here, but Neira couldn't find it in herself to worry. Vayne carried that burden willingly and she trusted in him to protect his own. She had other things to deal with and appreciated how they split the responsibilities. The learning curve was still steep but it never felt insurmountable, and while she and Vayne butted heads often enough, they always worked things out.

Nibiru was indeed a planet sadly empty of the calls and laughter of children, and a lack of females, something that would hopefully change over the next few decades. She and Vayne had made a start on that, as had the other couples from the *Tomodr*. Victoria had two little ones, and Sheera and Alondra were each expecting their second child. The rest of the women were already placed with lifemates and most of them were breeding. Funny how that concept didn't bother Neira anymore. It was hard to get worked up over something so natural when one's every need, desire and wish was immediately granted, and she hoped that never got old as more human women came to Nibiru to stay. Most of the male Shadalla she'd met were like Vayne—intensely dominant and no fool—and surely the depth of commitment would serve to eliminate a bond based on avarice.

Her feet were cold and she regretted not finding her slippers before moving quietly away to the nursery. She wore a nightgown because while Vayne insisted she remain uncovered in their bedroom, he wasn't inclined to let his entourage see her in that state. Her lips curved at his possessiveness and she hurried into their room.

"Are they asleep?" His deep voice startled her, not that she didn't expect him to be awake.

"They are. And hopefully for the night."

"We have their caregivers to tend to them, Neira."

It was the same discussion each and every time the triplets woke and called for her—or him. And each and every time one of them got up and took care of whatever reasons the children were awake. In fact, she knew he'd been hovering just out of sight while she soothed Alexi's childish bad dream and kissed his tears away, grateful the youngest triplet's cries hadn't woken Anika or Bella.

"I know we do. But I want to do it. As do you," she accused, climbing back into bed and putting her cold feet on his leg.

He manufactured a shudder, although she knew he barely felt the chill, and yanked her against him. Her sensitive breasts responded and her sex dampened at the feel of his solid cock flirting at the apex of her thighs. "I don't want you wearing yourself out."

"Hah. I'm waited on hand and foot. The occasional jaunt down the hall to the nursery won't wear me out. You're the one with a full schedule, ruling the planet." Organizing the screening and visitations of all the human women that Nibiru hosted was only part of his duties. "Yet you don't ignore the children."

She'd been astonished by how fulfilling the role of his lifemate and mother of his offspring, punctuated with appearances of political necessity and addressing those human women as she'd previously offered, was enough for her. And Vayne's gratitude was the only praise she required.

Exploring had been possible, and accompanied by Victoria, Sheera and Alondra—plus twenty or so trusted guards— they'd wandered at will. All the wives had followed their husband's edict that they cover themselves. None of the women had balked, aware of the simmering need of those Shadalla males on the streets of the city, the ones with no military training to instill exemplary self-control. Neira hoped all of them found their chosen, but it would take time. Perhaps even the belief it was possible would soon ease the desperation. Then there would be another sense of freedom for the females here.

"I see you continue to wish the last word, Neira." Vayne worked a hand beneath her night apparel. "And you're in my bed, clothed again."

The tearing of the really nice gown made her wince, but Vayne's expectations and desires hadn't relaxed, even after four Earth years and three children, even if the kids had all come at once. That first year had been one of adjustment, flavored with intimacy and that nonstop sex.

He maneuvered her on top of him, the light from the moons casting shards of illumination across his chest and handsome features. She crouched above him, her wet sex spread and nuzzling his cock, and she teased him with a slow glide. His growl made her do it again.

Hefting a breast in either hand, he leaned up to nibble at first one nipple, then the other and she shivered.

"Growing more and more sensitive, my chosen." He gave her a sly grin before suckling the right nipple and she moaned, involuntarily rocking her hips. When he gave the same treatment to the other, she gasped and tried to retreat. He immediately released her. "I won't tease you."

She leaned upright and traced a finger over the flat discs of his nipples, the tiny centers peaking with interest, then outlined the silvery remnants of his scar. His back was unblemished as Stenlor's skill had ordained, and for a moment she winced internally. Positive thoughts, being here with him, immediately replaced that dreadful time and she rocked against Vayne again. He had such a tendency to drive her pleasure to such heights it was no surprise she'd produced triplets. Her husband had crowed and strutted with pride at the news, assuming total responsibility for that fortune, of course.

"Why so pensive, my love?" His face creased with worry and she hurried to reassure him.

"Just thinking, reminiscing. Good thoughts. I love you."

"Then perhaps you might show me." His big hand cupped over her belly. "If this little one consents."

One. Singular. She carried only one fetus this time, although the second pregnancy had already curved her slender body, recovered with difficulty after the first births, to a very distinct and large shape. Not that she or Vayne cared. But he was afraid of crushing the baby, hence woman on top, something Neira relished with this dominant man. She hitched upward and gripped his fat cock, setting it at her entrance, and lowered herself in tiny increments. She swallowed a smile at the way her lifemate's lips set and his eyes narrowed as he instilled his self-control because of her slow pace. He stretched her most pleasurably, the walls of her pussy giving way grudgingly until he came up against her cervix. Neira clenched, experimentally, and Vayne groaned.

"Payback, my love? For your oh-so-sensitive nipples?" His fingers were on those tender buds in a blur of motion that took her breath and it was her turn to groan.

She was a needy, wanton sex fiend and had this alien male to thank. If she thought of it, he made it happen no matter how complicated her fantasy. And he was definitely creative in his own right, having had all those decades to hone his craft with the opportunities with otherworld females. Those sex toys had found their way to the bedroom and she'd been correct in thinking how experienced he was and how incredible those times would turn out to be. Not that any of them replaced the pleasure his cock brought her.

And beneath the physicality, where she could throw off all her burdens and surrender because Vayne would never let her fall, was the deep, abiding bond that melded their souls. Neira had never known this kind of connection but recognized it as love, that elusive four letter word, despite her past frantic attempts to deny herself.

Vayne let her set the pace as she rode him, and steadied her with his hands on her hips, occasionally using his amazing abdominal muscles to strain upward so he could access her breasts with his mouth. Between that intermittent sensation and working over his throbbing shaft, Neira swiftly climbed toward release. When she strained to reach the precipice, Vayne slid a finger over the top of her slit, above where they were joined so intimately, and flirted with the knot of nerves. The quick touch pushed her over with a shudder of her entire body and she felt all those tiny muscles inside her sheath strangle his cock. Vayne emitted a subdued roar and stiffened, then thrust in ragged tempo as he held her in place. She felt him come and bathe her with his seed and gloried in it.

Sagging over his chest, she enjoyed the final flutters of the release as their cum slipped down to signify the union. Vayne rubbed her back before resting a hand on one buttock.

"Glorious."

Neira was too spent to speak but made her lips pose a reasonable facsimile of a kiss against one hard pec.

He tugged a cover over them both to ward off any chill, and she sprawled on a very firm and heated mattress, reluctant to change position and lose him. Replete, Neira reflected and sighed with contentment.

"Heavy thoughts, my little warrior?"

"Good thoughts once again, my husband. Those responsible for the genetic weapon, the Shadalla's concern about extinction, my personal terrors—vanquished, all of them."

Vayne held her closer, his steady heartbeat lulling her into slumber.

The End

www.allysonyoung.com

Evernight Publishing

www.evernightpublishing.com